RENDEZVOUS IN CANNES

RENDEZVOUS IN CANNES

Jennifer Bohnet

CHIVERS

British Library Cataloguing in Publication Data available

This Large Print edition published by AudioGO Ltd, Bath, 2012.
Published by arrangement with Robert Hale Ltd.

U.K.   Hardcover   ISBN   978 1 4458 3770 3
U.K.   Softcover   ISBN   978 1 4458 3771 0

Printed and bound in Great Britain by
MPG Books Group Limited

RENDEZVOUS IN CANNES

CHAPTER 1

The day before she was due to fly to the South of France for the Cannes Film Festival, Anna Carson was in Somerset looking at a possible location for her latest film.

Marshland House lay at the end of a long drive flanked by flowering white rhododendron bushes. From the outside the brick-built Victorian mansion looked perfect. The agent had told her that the major part of the house was untouched since the nineteenth century and, importantly for the film, the basement kitchen still boasted its original fixtures.

Anna parked her rental car and glanced at her watch. Fifteen minutes before the agent was due. Time enough for her to have a quick look around the grounds on her own and take some photographs. Apart from the set designer needing some, she knew Leo would want to see photographs of the house and its location. A smile touched her lips as she thought about Leo.

Just four months ago she'd thought she was as happy as she was ever going to be. She had a successful career she enjoyed, her own home and money in the bank. Falling in love again hadn't been on her radar.

Then one evening at a restaurant, mutual friends had introduced her to Leo Hunter, a widower who worked in publishing. Unprepared for the feelings he'd stirred in her, she was wary when he telephoned the next day inviting her to the theatre but within days she knew she'd fallen unequivocally in love with him. The realization that Leo felt the same way about her had been, and still was, overwhelming.

Anna smiled at the memory of their first date; the way they'd just clicked. Within days they were acting like lovesick teenagers.

Unexpectedly too, she'd found herself being accepted as part of a family when Leo introduced her to his two grown-up children who unselfishly welcomed her presence in their father's life, pleased to see him happy again. With her own parents dead for years, it was a long time since she'd been part of a close family group.

Wandering around the grounds, Anna tried to banish all thoughts of Leo and concentrate instead on this latest film she

8

was working on, *In the Shadow of Mrs Beaton.* A costume drama based on the life of a little-known Victorian culinary expert, Mrs Agnes Marshall, even in pre-production days it was already stirring up a lot of interest. With a script written by a famous writer and a couple of big name stars lined up to play the principal roles, it was being tipped for box office success.

Her mobile rang while she was standing looking out over the lake that was part of the landscaped gardens to the rear of the house. Leo!

Taking a deep breath Anna answered the phone trying to speak naturally but try as she might, she'd never yet managed to stop her heart thumping or her hands shaking whenever she heard or saw Leo. This time was no different. She hadn't felt this way about anyone since those giddy days of her teenage love.

'Hi, how are you my darling? Have I told you how much I miss you when we're not together?'

'I'm fine, apart from missing you too. How about you?'

'I'm fine too. Is the house all the agent cracked it up to be?' Leo asked, knowing how important it was for Anna to find the right location.

'If the inside of the house is as good as the grounds, it will be perfect,' Anna told him. 'I'm glad I made the effort to come today. At least it's one less thing to worry about while I'm in Cannes.'

'Ah Cannes,' Leo said. There was a slight pause before he continued, 'I sincerely hope you know what you are doing, Anna my darling. Going back and raking up the past is not always a good idea.'

Even from two hundred miles away, Anna could hear the concern in his voice.

'Leo, I have no intention of "raking up the past" as you put it. I'm simply going to the film festival. I know I've managed to avoid it for the last thirty-odd years but it's time to lay the ghost now. Besides, how could I refuse to go this year? For the first time ever, a film I'm associated with is "In Competition" at Cannes. Both Rupert and Helen have asked me to be there for the film's premier.'

Picturing Leo and longing to feel his arms around her she said softly, 'Besides I can't wait to show off my handsome leading man on the red carpet. You are still joining me before the weekend aren't you?' she added anxiously. 'It will be our first holiday together.'

'I'll be there as early as I can,' Leo promised. 'Must go. I'll ring you tomorrow to make sure you've arrived safely in Cannes. Love you.'

'Love you too,' Anna smiled happily to herself, her hands trembling as she switched off her phone.

Looking out over the countryside, Anna sighed thoughtfully, her fingers toying with the chain of the gold locket she always wore around her neck. Was she tempting fate returning to Cannes? Would the errors of her past rear up and confront her — maybe even destroy what she had now? Leo hadn't mentioned marriage in so many words yet, but Anna suspected, hoped, he would soon.

Standing in the grounds of Marshland House that afternoon, Anna resolved to talk to Leo again about her past. All of it. He deserved to know the whole truth.

What she had told him so far had been the merest skeleton of events. Until she knew him better she'd been afraid to tell him the whole story but now she was confident of her strong love for him, and his for her, she wanted him to know the complete story. She was determined to be totally honest with Leo. It was the only way.

Hearing car tyres scrunch along the gravel on the drive, Anna made her way round to the front of the house where the agent was parking his car alongside hers.

An hour later as the agent left for another appointment, Anna switched on the car radio and sat for a few moments writing up her notes. Inside, the house had been everything she'd hoped it would be and she'd instructed the agent to draw up a contract to allow filming to begin there in the Autumn and send it to her office. Now she could go to Cannes and enjoy the festival.

Pressing the shut down button on her laptop before sliding it into its case, she turned up the volume on the radio to hear the last item of the news bulletin.

'Some news just in. The respected French film-maker Philippe Cambone has died in America. Responsible for some of the biggest blockbuster movies of the twentieth century he was recently awarded an industry lifetime achievement Bafta which was to be presented at this week's Cannes film Festival.'

Automatically Anna reached out and turned off the radio before closing her eyes and leaning back against her seat as a wave of numbness and desolation flooded her body.

How could Philippe Cambone die on the eve of her return to Cannes?

■ ■ ■ ■

'I'm sorry to land on you last minute like this,' Daisy said, paying off the taxi driver who'd driven her from the airport, before turning to face Poppy, her sister. 'But I really couldn't face sharing a small apartment with Marcus and his cronies and there's no hope of finding an empty hotel room in Cannes this week. Besides, I'd far rather stay here with you.'

'You know you're more than welcome anytime,' Poppy said. 'Just so long as you don't mind camping out with Tom and me in the old cottage.'

'Hi Tom. How you doing?' Daisy gave her young nephew a high five before hugging her sister.

'So, who have you rented the villa to for the Festival? Pleeease tell me Johnny Depp and his family are going to be in residence.'

'Sorry to disappoint you but the villa has been booked in the name of Anna Carson. I've never heard of her, but that doesn't mean anything,' Poppy answered. 'You know what I'm like, haven't got a clue about celebrities.'

'Anna Carson,' Daisy said thoughtfully. 'Nope it's not a name that rings any bells with me either. Obviously not gossip column material. Where's Dan by the way?'

'Convenient business trip to America. You know how he hates the whole festival scene. When I was asked to rent the villa for a sum that will pay the mortgage for a couple of years, he said, "Go for it, but I won't be here!"'

'Fair enough I suppose,' Daisy said, knowing her brother-in-law's views on film-stars and so-called 'A list' personalities. 'Makes life easier for you that way as well. When does this Anna Carson get here and take up residence?'

'Tomorrow afternoon,' Poppy answered. 'She's asked me to arrange for a car to collect her.'

'So we've still got the place to ourselves this evening and tomorrow morning,' Daisy said. 'We can at least have a swim when I get back tonight. Thought I'd go and collect my press pack and accreditation pass this evening instead of in the morning when every hack in town will be down there,' she added. 'I told Marcus the photographer I'd see him there in about an hour.'

'Let's get you settled in the cottage then,' Poppy said. 'Tom and I are sharing the bedroom — I've put a clic-clac bed on the mezzanine for you. Hope that's OK,' Poppy glanced anxiously at her sister.

'It'll be fine,' Daisy assured her and followed her sister down the narrow path past the swimming pool towards the corner of the garden where the cottage was hidden away from view.

Once a home for the full-time housekeeper and gardener who looked after the villa, the cottage had fallen into disrepair and when Poppy and Dan bought the property two years before, the cottage, even more than the villa, was in dire need of some tender loving care. Today was the first time Daisy had seen the result of all Poppy's hard work.

'Wow, what a transformation,' she said, looking around the sitting room. 'First the villa and now this place. You should have been an interior designer — you've got such a good eye. I love the Provençal colour scheme in here,' she added, looking around the sitting room with its terracotta floor tiles and yellow and blue furnishings.

With French doors and windows down two sides, the room had a spacious feel about it and Poppy's colour scheme and furniture gave the room a welcoming, homely feel.

Poppy led the way up a flight of wooden stairs in the far corner to the mezzanine whose railing ran like a minstrel's galley along the width of the room.

Daisy put her laptop bag on the chest of drawers standing between two varnished doors and her suitcase on the floor.

'I'm hoping this will give you enough privacy,' Poppy said, pulling open a decorative wicker screen that would hide from view the bed she'd placed at the end of the mezzanine.

'That's the bathroom and this is the bedroom,' Poppy continued opening one of the doors. 'I've left some hangers for you to use in the wardrobe so you can at least unpack. These drawers are empty,' she said indicating the chest. 'I've put towels and things out for you in the bathroom and —'

'Poppy, stop fussing. You're sounding more and more like Mum,' Daisy said. 'It's all fine. Incidentally have you spoken to Mum recently?'

Poppy nodded. 'She and Dad are hoping to come over at the end of the month. Apparently Dad's won some tickets to see the Monaco Grand Prix. Goodness only knows where I'm expected to put them the first night — Anna Carson doesn't leave until the next day. Sandwich?'

'Please and then I must think about walking down to Cannes.'

Downstairs, in the kitchen Poppy had created in what had originally been a lean-to conservatory, Daisy picked up Oscar, Poppy's fat ginger and white cat and absently stroked him as she looked out over the garden.

'Is Anna C staying on her own?'

Poppy shrugged as she concentrated on making sandwiches.

'Some of the time. She's asked me to make up the bed in the master bedroom and one of the guest rooms but just to leave bedding in the other two rooms in case she has guests. She's hoping her partner will arrive before the weekend. He's hiring a car at the airport so at least I don't have to worry about organizing transport for him.'

'Did she sound okay when you spoke to her? Or does she have "show biz attitude"?' Daisy rolled her eyes in mock horror.

Poppy laughed. 'No, she sounded really nice and down to earth. Let's take this out into the garden,' and she led the way out to the swing seat under the shade of the linden tree.

'So what's this photographer Marcus like? Replacement material?' Poppy said hopefully.

Daisy laughed. 'Honestly Poppy. He's just someone from work. I don't really know him properly. Anyway I'm not sure I'm ready for another relationship yet.'

'Daisy, it's been six months since Ben upped and left you for the delights of Australia. Life goes on. It's about time you found someone else.'

Daisy nodded, wondering whether to tell Poppy about the letter she'd stuffed in her bag and decided she'd leave it until later, when they'd have more time to talk about it together. 'I know. But I'm quite enjoying being single. Anyway I don't think Marcus is my type. Far too flamboyant. But talking of Marcus, I'd better get going.'

'Bring him back for supper if you like,' Poppy offered. 'I'd like to meet him. Give him the third degree and see if he has potential as a boyfriend for my little sister,' she added.

'No way,' Daisy said. 'You and I are having a girlie evening before the film festival takes over my life for the next fortnight. Right, I'd better dash. See you later.'

Cannes was in countdown to festival time as Daisy walked along the bord de mer and made her way towards the old port and the Palais des Festivals.

The events of the past few days had happened so fast she could scarcely believe she was officially here as a journalist at one of

18

the biggest annual show business events in the world. She must remember to send Damien a postcard thanking him for breaking his leg two days ago.

The palm tree–lined streets were more chaotic than usual, with nose to tail traffic stuttering its way around double parked vans and lorries busy unloading last minute supplies to various exhibition venues and traders.

Impatient gun toting gendarmes, standing in front of 'route barre' signs, directed frustrated motorists down narrow streets they knew would take them in the opposite direction to where they wanted to go.

Workers were busy sweeping and checking the condition of the red carpet that now covered the most famous flight of twenty-four steps in the world.

Dodging the crowds that were milling aimlessly around hoping to rub shoulders with the few stars already in town, Daisy made her way round to the back of the Palais des Festivals. Marcus was leaning against the railings watching the crowds on the beach, his official photographer pass already strung around his neck, his camera at the ready.

'You settled in all right at your sister's place?' Marcus asked.

19

Daisy nodded. 'Where do I go to register?'

Marcus pointed to a door in the Palais. 'Through there. You'll be ages — French paperwork and chaotic bureaucracy is at its best in there. I'll wait for you in The UK Film Centre Pavilion over in the Village International,' he said. 'We'll go for a coffee afterwards and try to map out a plan of campaign.'

'Plan of campaign?'

'As well as a daily report and photos, Bill wants us to try to unearth some unusual stories — a scandal would be good, he says,' Marcus shrugged. 'You know what editors are like — always wanting a scoop.'

Marcus was right. It was nearly two hours before Daisy escaped from the Accreditation Centre, her press pass finally around her neck and clutching a mountain of booklets and other assorted festival papers. When she eventually tracked Marcus down in the Film Centre marquee he was with a group of men — all photographers, Daisy guessed from the amount of camera paraphernalia surrounding them.

'Hi guys, this is Daisy my new partner in crime from the paper. I'll see you lot later. Daisy and I have to talk.'

Marcus picked up his large canvas bag and Daisy followed him across the road to a pavement café in front of Square Brougham where they managed to grab a vacant corner table.

'Deux cafés au lait s'il vous plaît,' Marcus ordered, raising his voice to be heard above the noise of a group of vocal Italians at the next table, some Russians who'd clearly been there for some time sampling the house rosé and a nearby crowd of Americans who seemed intent on taking over the place. A Japanese tourist was busy videoing the scene.

'Hope he's got his sound switched on,' Daisy said. 'I've never heard so many languages all at once.'

'Heard the news about Philippe Cambone?' Marcus asked, as the waiter put their coffees on the table.

Daisy shook her head. 'The big shot film director? What's happened?'

'Died of a heart attack. There's going to be some sort of tribute later in the week — the powers to be haven't decided what yet. Do you know much about Cambone?'

'Only that he was French, was one of the top directors, wasn't married,' she glanced at Marcus. 'Wasn't gay was he?'

Marcus shrugged. 'If he was, it was a well kept secret. Had a reputation of loving women but wouldn't commit to one. Any-

21

way, I expect they've got all the info they need back at the office but maybe you could do a couple of paragraphs about how the news has been received down here? Cannes was his home town. Maybe interview a few people who knew him? You know the score — find a human interest angle. The school he went to; name of his first love etc. etc.'

Marcus drained his coffee and pushed the cup and saucer away before asking, 'You got a press conference tomorrow?'

'Not tomorrow. I'm hoping to get to a screening in the morning and then I'm having lunch with a friend of Poppy's who works for Chanel. She's promised to give me the lowdown on some of the accessories and clothes they'll be lending the stars. So I should have a spare hour in the morning to try and see if I can find someone to talk about Philippe Cambone. Then in the afternoon I'll file my first daily report.'

'Don't forget to keep your ears open for any juicy gossip,' Marcus said. 'It's what this place is good for — and Bill is keen to hear some of it.'

'As you're an old hand at this lark, where's the best place to hang out to catch the gossip? See people?'

'Any of the cafés and bars in town. This place is good,' Marcus said glancing around.

22

'Occasionally some of the up-and-coming stars like to come down here and hang out with the boules players over there. Too much security these days for the famous ones to do that, unfortunately. Mind you, if Jack Nicholson is in town he's known to like an early morning stroll along the Croisette by himself.'

Marcus stood up. 'Right I'm off. Want to come to a party tomorrow night? I've got tickets for Bruno's bash. It should be a good starting place for gossip. Meet me after the evening screening and we'll go together. Ten thirty outside the Petit Majestic — it's on the corner of rue Victor Cousin.'

'Who's Bruno?'

'Big name down here. Knows everybody who is anybody. Good contact.'

'Thanks. I'll definitely try to be there.' Daisy hesitated. She really did want to spend the evening alone with her sister but felt she ought to at least make the offer for Marcus to join them. 'Are you doing anything tonight? Poppy and I are planning a girlie evening but if you'd like to come to supper? I warn you, you're likely to get the third degree from my sister.'

Marcus shook his head. 'Thanks but I've arranged to meet the guys for a quick drink and then a reasonably early night. Doubt that I'll see bed much before three or four a.m. most days while the festival is on. Expect you'll find the same once you get into the swing of things.'

Unexpectedly he lent forward and kissed her cheek. 'When in France and all that,' he said. He picked up his camera gear. 'If you need me urgently, you've got my mobile number and you'll invariably find me in the paparazzi scrum at the side of the red ·carpet. And we've got a definite date for dinner one evening before the festival ends — either the Carlton Terrace or the Palm Beach. You choose. Bill can pick up the tab! See you tomorrow night. Ciao.' And he sauntered off in the direction of Palm Beach. Thoughtfully Daisy watched him go. Well that was definitely the most unromantic dinner date invite she'd ever had, but dinner at the Carlton might be good.

Daisy gathered her things together and headed off in the opposite direction. Passing the busy pizza restaurant on the corner brought back memories of the last time she'd had a pizza in there. The four of them, Poppy, Dan, Ben and herself had been celebrating the villa's renovation being finished. She'd been so happy that night. She and Ben had even talked about the possibility of moving to France and restoring a cottage themselves.

Back home a week later her world had fallen apart when Ben told her it was all over between them. Apparently all the talk that night of getting a mortgage and settling down together had freaked him out.

'I'm not ready for that sort of commitment, Daisy. I need some space.' The space he needed was in Australia. Sydney to be precise.

How ironic then that his first letter should arrive as she left to catch her flight down here where they'd been happy. Unsure of how to reply Daisy had stuffed the letter into her bag. She'd get Poppy to read it later and see if she had any ideas about Ben's suggestion.

Standing with several people waiting for a green pedestrian crossing light on the bord de mer, Daisy smiled at a little girl waiting with a tall man.

'Nat, d'you think Daddy will be at the house when we get back?' the girl asked hopefully, looking up at the man.

'Maybe Cindy. His plane should have landed an hour ago and an official car was picking him up to bring him straight here.'

'Good,' Cindy said. 'He can take me to the park tomorrow.'

'Sorry, Cindy, I think you'll have to make

25

do with me. Daddy and Mummy are going to be really busy for the next week. That's why they've asked me to look after you.'

Daisy smiled sympathetically as the man looked up and saw her watching. He returned the smile but didn't speak.

Just then the lights changed and the small crowd surged forward. Once across the road, Daisy stopped on the pretence of rummaging for something in her bag and let the man and girl walk past her, curious to see where they were going.

It was a hundred yards or so before they stopped in front of a pair of large wrought iron gates where the man pressed a security button high in the wall and spoke into the intercom.

One of the dark green gates with its golden spikes on top swung slowly open giving pedestrian access and the two disappeared from sight into a private garden. Daisy caught a glimpse of immaculate grounds, and a villa covered with bougainvillea before the gate snapped shut behind them.

Daisy strolled on past and ten minutes later she and Poppy were sat at the table under the loggia, with a glass of wine to hand, thumbing through the various film magazines and trade papers Daisy had collected in Cannes.

'So, you still enjoying being a journalist?'

Daisy hesitated long enough for her sister to throw her a curious glance, before saying slowly, 'Chasing after news stories is losing its appeal. Anyway, I mightn't have a job much longer. There are rumours flying around at work about major redundancies in the next few months. So, I'm seriously thinking of going freelance and finding some sort of specialism.' She shrugged.

'I could even move over here. Live with you while I find something. I still like the idea of renovating a place.'

'You could have the cottage,' Poppy said. 'I know Dan would be pleased for me to have you near when he's away — his business trips seem to becoming more and more frequent.' She poured some more wine.

'Any idea what you'd specialize in?'

'Lifestyle? Property? Quite fancy the idea of getting to look around posh houses. Incidentally there's this gorgeous belle époque villa below you that must have so much history attached to it. Dark green gates with gold spikes. D'you know it? Saw a little girl and her minder disappearing in there earlier.'

'If it's the one I think you mean,' Poppy said, 'then it's someone with either a lot of money or good connections staying there. It's one of the original grand nineteenth-century villas along that road. It was bought last year by some Russian who's spent a fortune renovating it. Now apparently it's the latest word in twenty-first-century opulence. Available only to those with the necessary funds.'

'Well, "Daddy" is clearly some festival VIP to warrant an official car. Shall have to do a bit of sleuthing tomorrow I think,' Daisy said. 'The little girl's name was Cindy — not that usual a name. Somebody is bound to know who her VIP father is. Maybe she's got a famous mother too.'

'Don't any of your official booklets and papers have potted biographies of important people attending the festival?' Poppy asked. 'Have a look while I go and check Tom is asleep and fetch another bottle of rosé.'

When she returned, Daisy waved a booklet at her. 'No luck with my mystery VIP but I've found your Anna Carson. She's a well respected production designer, worked on lots of films over the years. Apparently this is her first visit to Cannes.'

Later, sitting on the edge of her put-u-up bed balancing her laptop on her knees, Daisy updated her 'To Do list'. Tomorrow she'd a) go to a screening b) find someone to interview about Philippe Cambone c) talk to the girl from Chanel d) write up her first report e) try to uncover a scoop for Bill and f) go to Bruno's party.

She smiled ruefully to herself as she wrote 'uncover a scoop'. She didn't doubt there were lots of secret scandals floating around in a place like Cannes but whether she was capable of unearthing one was something else. Maybe she'd overhear something at Bruno's party.

CHAPTER 2

'I'm sitting at a sea-front café, croissant and coffee to hand, watching Cannes come to life on the first full day of the festival. The morning sky is the brilliant blue that gives this stretch of the Riviera its other name, the Cote d'Azur, and the forecast is for a sunny day.

'All around me there are giant billboards advertising the films that will be screening here over the next few days. Although only 7.15 a.m. there is a general sense of bustle everywhere. Queues are already forming outside boulangeries, espresso machines are hissing into life, squirting the dark, strong liquid the French call coffee, into small cups.

'People are arriving bleary-eyed back at their hotels and apartments hoping to catch a few hours' sleep after partying the night away. Others, bright eyed and with a spring in their step, are on their way out to the first breakfast meetings of the festival.'

Daisy took a swig of her coffee and a bite of croissant before continuing to speak the first of her daily reports into her small voice recorder.

'I've collected all the daily trade magazines, signed up for a press conference tomorrow morning with a famous star — more of that later in the week — and now I'm off to view my first early morning screening. With over one hundred and twenty films to be shown during the festival, things start early around here.'

Daisy pressed the save button and switched off the recorder. She'd add some more to it after lunch with the fashion assistant who had promised to explain how the stars managed to acquire the necessary glitz for film premiers and type it up later back at Poppy's. After drinking the rest of her coffee she set off for the Theatre Bazin on the third floor of the Palais, where many of the press screenings would be held during the festival — far away from the glamour of the red carpet.

Emerging three hours later, her head buzzing from both the film and the Q & A session with the film-makers that had followed, Daisy joined the lunchtime crowds that were thronging the Croisette: tourists

and locals enjoying the presence of entertainers and starlets strutting their stuff —
anxious to catch the eye of any movie maker
that might be around.

As she walked, intriguing snippets of
conversation floated in the air around her.

'Sharon was really upset when Michael
gave the part to . . .'

'Gosh yes, a ticket to the Vanity Fair party
would be to die for. Any chance of . . .'

'No. We can't meet there. It's too risky.
What if we were seen?'

Marcus was right; there was gossip everywhere. And surely that was Tom Hanks over
there talking to Bruce Willis? Wandering
through the crowds she wondered again
about the possibility of chasing down a
scoop for the paper. She just wasn't that
keen on investigative journalism. As she'd
told Poppy, she much preferred to write feel
good stories about people rather than ones
that besmirched them.

Lingering near the roundabout she saw
Cindy riding around happily on one of the
carousel horses, the tall man standing to
one side attentively watching. He smiled in
acknowledgement at Daisy when he saw
her, before turning as the carousel slowed
to a stop and helping Cindy off.

'Come on, let's go for those pizzas.

Mummy said she'd meet us there and maybe Daddy as well.'

So Daddy had arrived then, Daisy thought, wishing she could follow them and see who Mummy and Daddy were. But it was time for her to learn how the stars managed their haute couture appearances.

It was past three o'clock when she arrived back at the villa intending to write up her notes, finish her report and do some internet research on Philippe Cambone. Having failed to unearth anyone locally who'd known the director and was willing to talk to her, the internet seemed her only option. With luck too, she'd be able to grab some sleep before heading back down into Cannes for the first evening red carpet screening and then on to Bruno's party with Marcus.

Poppy was on the telephone as she walked into the cottage.

'Well I'm glad you're très desolé but it doesn't help me this afternoon, does it?' Poppy slammed the phone down before turning to face Daisy.

'Can you believe it. The car people have double booked and they're "very sorry" but they are unable to meet Anna Carson this afternoon.' Poppy ran her hands through her hair distractedly. 'What on earth am I going to do? It'll be impossible to find anyone else at this short notice.'

'I shouldn't worry. I expect she'll just grab a taxi,' Daisy said.

'But Anna's expecting to be met. I've got no way of telling her to take a taxi. My first booking for the villa and this happens.'

'What time is her flight landing?' Daisy asked.

'In an hour,' Poppy said looking at her watch.

'I can look after Tom — where is he, by the way? And you can collect Anna in your car.'

'Would you? Oh, no that won't work,' Poppy sighed. 'He's at school until three thirty this afternoon and they don't know you so they won't let him come with you before I've officially introduced you.' She looked at Daisy. 'I don't suppose you?'

'Poppy, you know how much I hate driving down here,' Daisy said sighing. 'But okay. Give me the flight details and the car keys and I'll go and meet your Anna Carson.'

Anna was relieved when the plane finally landed at Nice airport, fifty minutes late. It had been an uncomfortable flight and she couldn't wait to collect her luggage and meet up with the car she'd ordered to take her to the Villa Flora.

The Arrivals hall when she walked through was crowded. Official looking chauffeurs were everywhere, holding up boards with various names on them, none of them hers. As people were shepherded off to their transport and the waiting crowds thinned slightly, Anna stood there at a loss to know what to do.

'Anna Carson?' a voice at her elbow said hesitantly.

'Yes,' she said turning to face a young woman, holding a piece of paper with 'Anna Carson' scrawled across it.

'Hi, I'm Daisy. I'm afraid there was a difficulty with your hire car and Poppy asked me to meet you.'

'Oh thank goodness. Being so late I was afraid I was stranded,' Anna said smiling. Following Daisy as she led the way through the car park, Anna listened as Daisy explained what had happened.

'So, instead of a proper chauffeur and a limo, you've got me and my sister's run around,' Daisy said apologetically as she opened the boot and put Anna's case inside.

'I'm just grateful to be met,' Anna said. 'I'm not that fond of limos anyway. I like sitting in the front passenger seat and official chauffeurs aren't too keen on that.'

As Daisy concentrated on finding her way out of the car park and back to the autoroute, Anna sat quietly looking out of the window.

When Daisy let out a muttered curse she said, 'Something wrong?'

'I've missed the autoroute entry slip-road. Do you mind if we go back along the bord de mer instead? At least I know my way then.'

'The scenic route will be fine,' Anna said. 'Do you live down here with your sister?'

'No. I'm staying with her for the festival. I'm a journalist,' Daisy said. 'It's my first time covering the Cannes Festival.'

Waiting in a queue of traffic Daisy looked across at Anna. 'I gather this is your first festival too?'

'What makes you say that?' Anna said surprised.

'Your bio in one of the trade papers says although you've been in the industry for some time, you've never been to Cannes before,' Daisy said.

'Never had a film make its premier here before,' Anna answered.

'Your film *Future Promises* is showing at the weekend, isn't it? I expect you're looking forward to walking up the infamous steps?'

'Think so. I'm not used to being in the glare of the spotlight,' Anna said. 'To be truthful I find the whole thing rather daunting. Much rather be in the background of things.' She smiled. 'So long as my partner Leo manages to get here in time, I'll be fine.'

'Personally I'm amazed at how large the whole festival is,' Daisy said. 'The number of trade stands is huge and everyone seems to be networking like mad.'

'My favourite festival is Deauville,' Anna said. 'Less trade, far more about the films. Same with Venice. But Cannes is the big one. The important one in the industry.'

'The public come to see the stars but people in the film industry simply want to do deals. At least that's what Marcus the photographer I'm working with tells me. Is your company exhibiting here?' Daisy asked.

Anna nodded. 'Yes. I have to show my face at a couple of meetings with some American clients. Where are we now?'

'Skirting Antibes. A few more minutes and we'll be passing the celebrated Eden Roc Hotel where I'm told the best people stay and the best parties are held. Another ten minutes and we should be on the outskirts of Cannes.'

'Spectacular views,' Anna said looking out across the bay as they drove down the hill.

While Daisy concentrated on the narrow winding coast road as it made its way around the Cap d'Antibes and on through Juan-les-Pins, Anna enjoyed the changing scenery.

The sudden whoosh of a TGV rushing past on the railway line that followed the road as it approached Golf-Juan made her jump. Approaching Cannes the traffic began to build up and soon they were reduced to a crawl.

Anna saw Daisy glance at the dashboard clock before saying, 'At this rate it's going to take us ages to get to the villa.'

'Have you got things lined up to do this evening?' Anna asked, guiltily aware her plane being so late had probably created a few problems for Daisy.

Daisy nodded. 'I've got to finish and file my first report for the newspaper, do a spot of internet research on this big director who's just died, take a look at tonight's stars on the red carpet and then I get to go to a party later.' She glanced at Anna.

'Don't suppose you knew this Philippe Cambone did you? Work with him even? Any info — personal anecdotes or anything — would be gratefully received.'

'No I never worked with Philippe Cambone so unfortunately I can't help you with any anecdotes that you won't find on the internet.' Anna turned to look out of her passenger window, effectively finishing the conversation.

'That's a shame,' Daisy said disappointed. 'There's not a lot of info out there. Seems Mr Cambone was a very private person. Oh good the traffic is clearing, we're on the move again.'

'Are we going via the Croisette?' Anna asked.

'Only so far. The police will have barricaded the road before we reach The Bunker, ready for the evening screening.'

'The Bunker?'

'Local name for the Festival des Palais,' Daisy explained. 'We'll have to take a right and go round the back streets. Hopefully it won't add too much time to the journey.'

With a silent Anna beside her Daisy concentrated on her driving and a few minutes later turned into the villa drive. Poppy, hearing the electric gates opening, was waiting by the front door to greet them.

Daisy turned to Anna. 'Poppy will look after you now. Hope you don't think me terribly rude but I must dash and try and catch up with a few things before I walk down to Cannes. I expect we'll bump into each other over the next few days, either here or in town. Enjoy the festival.'

'Thanks for meeting me, Daisy. Do come and have glass of wine with me when you're not so frantic.'

'I'd like that,' Daisy said. 'Ciao.' And Daisy ran down the path to the cottage leaving Anna with Poppy.

'This way,' Poppy said, taking Anna's suitcase and leading the way into the Villa Floral.

'I've never rented the villa out before,' Poppy said. 'I hope everything is okay for you,' she added anxiously as she showed Anna around.

'Please don't worry,' Anna said. 'I'm sure you've thought of everything. It looks fantastic.'

Long buttercup yellow curtains hung either side of the French doors and windows. A bookcase lined the wall alongside the fireplace and a small glass table holding some glossy magazines and candles was placed between a couple of inviting cream sofas with deep feather cushions. A large terracotta pot filled with lavender stood in the fireplace infusing the whole villa with its perfume.

'There's a welcome box in the kitchen with a few basics: cheese, eggs, baguette, tomatoes, milk, butter. And there's a bottle of rosé in the fridge,' Poppy said, going into the kitchen with its views out over the patio towards the swimming pool.

Just then Tom ran into the kitchen. 'Mummy, can I have one last swim before Mrs Carson gets here? Oh, you're here already,' he added seeing Anna.

'Tom, please say how do you do to Ms Carson,' Poppy said. 'And then go back to the cottage. I'll be there in a moment to get your supper.'

Anna held her hand out for Tom to shake. 'How do you do, Tom? My name is Anna.'

'How do you do, Anna,' Tom said seriously. 'Do you like swimming?'

'I do indeed and I guess you do too.'

Tom nodded. 'Only now I can't. Mummy says the pool is yours while you're here and nobody else can use it 'cause you're paying for it.'

'Tom!' Poppy exclaimed.

Anna bent down to talk to Tom. 'Ah. Well I expect my friends will be coming for a swim, so if you're my friend I can invite you and Mummy won't mind then.'

'Now?' Tom asked hopefully.

'No.' Poppy answered before Anna could say anything. 'Anna has to settle in this evening. Besides it's almost your bedtime. Cottage,' and she held the kitchen door open for a reluctant to leave Tom.

'I'm sorry,' Poppy said, embarrassed. 'I'll keep him out of your way while you're here. I'll take him to the beach so he can swim.'

'Poppy, it's not a problem. Please let him come for a swim. I like having children around.'

'If you're sure. Now, I think I'd better leave you in peace to settle in. If you want anything, just come over to the cottage. Bye for now.'

Closing the door behind Poppy, Anna went upstairs and pulled her swimming costume out of her case. The pool was too tempting to resist. The unpacking could wait.

The water was warm and inviting and Anna swam ten lengths before turning over and floating lazily on her back, allowing her mind to wander over the upcoming days.

So far her diary contained just four definite appointments: The gala screening of *Future Promises* at the weekend; a meeting with her company's French representative; dinner with the American producer who was keen to come on board for the Agnes Marshall film. The fourth date was the party here at the villa she was planning to hold during the second week of the festival — when Leo had arrived. She'd need to talk to

Poppy about the catering for it. The fifth appointment 'Ring Philippe' would never be made now.

A moon was rising in the darkening sky as she made her way indoors to shower and finish unpacking. Hanging the evening gown she intended wearing for the weekend premier in the spacious wardrobe, her attention was caught by a series of postcard size photographs grouped together on the bedroom wall.

Moving closer she saw that some were sepia in colour and showed the beach and harbour before the Croisette was built. Another showed the old casino on the edge of the harbour with figures in Edwardian costume stiffly posing outside.

The one that caught Anna's attention was more recent; a black and white photo of a large building with square flat columns and a short flight of steps leading up to the entrance. Even as she bent closer to read the faded lettering at the base of the card, Anna had already recognized it as the old 'Festival des Palais, Cannes'.

It had been a lovely building, she thought affectionately. So different to the concrete 'Bunker' she'd glimpsed before Daisy had turned off the Croisette. Her mobile phone rang as she finished arranging the rest of her clothes in the closet. Pressing the answer button with shaking fingers she said, 'Hello Leo,' as she ran downstairs to the kitchen.

'Anna, my darling. How was the flight?'

'Terrible,' Anna answered. 'But I'm here now. Villa Flora is delightful. A real find. You're going to love it.'

'Are you going out for dinner tonight?'

'No. I've just had a swim and I'm about to indulge in a baguette and some cheese with a glass of rosé that Poppy very kindly left for me, before having an early night. Tomorrow I'll wander down to Cannes and show my face. The office is doing all the major stuff — I just have to show up a couple of times and do as I'm told.'

'Haven't done any sightseeing yet then?'

Anna laughed. 'Leo, I've barely got here. I'll probably have a bit of a mooch around tomorrow, if the crowds aren't too large. I've got to do some food shopping anyway. How are things at your end?' she asked, knowing that Leo was spending the night with his daughter and her new husband. 'How's Alison?'

'She's blooming,' Leo laughed down the line. 'Literally. Told me tonight she's making me a grandfather before Christmas!'

'Oh Leo, how wonderful. Do give her my love.'

'I will. Speak tomorrow. Goodnight, my darling.'

Thoughtfully Anna prepared herself a supper tray with the goodies from the welcome basket, poured herself a glass of wine and carried it out to a small pool-side table. Sonar garden lights placed randomly around were illuminating the terrace and garden.

Sitting there, absently fingering her gold locket Anna allowed herself to dream about her future with Leo. What would life be like as a married woman? Having a ready made family?

Carefully she slipped the locket with its chain over her head and pressed the catch. Two photographs, a few strands of hair, were nestling together in the interior. Anna gently stroked the hair as she looked at the photos. For years she'd kept the photos, both as a memento and as a link to her past, always hopeful that maybe one day her secret dream would come true. Then, she planned to replace the photos with new, modern versions. Tonight though, brushing a tear away, Anna realized she had to accept the facts. Too much time had passed. She'd left it too late.

CHAPTER 3

After collecting Anna, Daisy had no time to
do more than a quick internet search for
information on Philippe Cambone — which
yielded very little of interest. Mainly the
titles of the major films he'd been involved
with. Not a hint of any scandal which was
what Daisy had secretly been hoping for. As
Marcus said, he'd obviously liked the ladies
as there were lots of publicity shots taken
over the years at various festivals and film
premiers though rarely with the same companion hanging from his arm.

No real gossip anywhere about his private
life, other than he was a keen sailor and kept
a boat in his home port of Cannes. Maybe
she could locate that and get Marcus to take
a photo. She sighed as she shut down her
laptop. She'd have another go tomorrow;
there had to be something out there about
him.

A quick shower and Daisy dithered over

what to wear that was practical for the first part of the evening but would look dressy enough for Bruno's party later, which she knew would almost certainly be full of skinny women dressed to impress. Her normal jeans and tee-shirt definitely wouldn't do. In the end she decided on her black velvet trouser suit with a silver spaghetti strap glittery top under the jacket.

'You look great,' Poppy assured her. 'Have fun.'

'Don't know what time I'll be back. I promise to creep in as quietly as I can.'

Daisy took a short cut down through Le Suquet hoping to miss the crowds. A ploy that worked until she reached the top of rue Saint Antoine. From there on the place was buzzing with people out intent on enjoying themselves. Although still early, the restaurants were beginning to fill with the first diners of the evening, and Daisy caught tantalizing whiffs of food being cooked as she passed the various eateries.

What Daisy privately nicknamed the 'men in suits' with their official Festival passes hanging around their necks, and their loud important voices, were out in force busy networking on their BlackBerrys and laptops setting up deals to be finalized later in the week.

Gendarmes and security men were everywhere, nonchalantly watching the proceedings but alert to any possible trouble erupting. The paparazzi, ten deep around the Palais des Festivals steps, were busy photographing the stars arriving for the evening screening.

Daisy squeezed into a space next to a step ladder that had been positioned on the middle of the road island separating the Croisette from the bord de mer. The woman sitting on top of it looked down and said, 'You're welcome to stand on the bottom for a better view.'

'Great. Thanks,' Daisy said.

'First Festival? I've been every year for the past ten,' the woman continued not waiting for an answer. 'Can't stay away. Know now to bring this and get here early for the best view. Oooh look there's my favourite, George Clooney. Fancy a coffee, George?'

By the time all the stars had arrived and gone up the red carpet, it was dusk and all the lights were on. Declining her new friend's offer of going for a drink, Daisy opted instead to have a wander around the Village International while she waited to meet up with Marcus.

It proved to be a long wait. The evening screening had run on late and then Marcus

48

had wanted to get some shots of the celebrities being whisked off to a private yacht for a champagne party. It was almost midnight before they began to make their way through the crowds still milling around on the Croisette to the party that Marcus had invites for.

There was no mistaking their own party venue as they turned into a narrow street off rue d'Antibes: blazing lights and pounding music and a crush of people queuing to enter the building.

'I'm not sure I'm up for this,' Daisy said, stifling a yawn as they joined the tail-end of the queue. 'It's been a long day. Might just call a taxi and go home.'

'Come on Daisy, don't be a wimp, it's only the first day of the festival,' Marcus said. 'I did warn you about the late nights. Bruno's a good contact for you, he knows lots of people — you never know who might be inside.'

'OK. But it's your fault if I fall down asleep.'

'Not a chance with this racket going on,' Marcus said taking her by the hand and leading her into the building as the security men took their tickets. 'Now let's mingle and see if we can find our host.'

Bruno, when they eventually located him

holding court on a first floor balcony, welcomed Marcus enthusiastically and kissed Daisy on the cheek when Marcus introduced her.

'Bruno, you knew Philippe Cambone well, didn't you?' Marcus asked. 'Daisy's writing a piece for the paper.'

Bruno nodded. 'We go way back. He was best man at my wedding. He's my son's godfather. Such a shock.' Bruno bit his lip, clearly upset.

'He was supposed to be here tonight helping me host this bash. Instead I have to help arrange a tribute but his family are being difficult.'

'How?' Daisy asked.

'They say it's a private matter and Philippe wouldn't have wanted a fuss,' Bruno sighed. 'But what they don't seem to realize is how big a name he is, was, in the industry. We can't just ignore his passing. It's not possible.'

Bruno took a sip of champagne from the glass he was holding. 'His brother, Jacques, says it's complicated. That there are other people to be considered — presumably he means Agnes, their mother. At nearly one hundred the news has made her ill. So everything has to be low key to avoid upsetting her further. All Jacques will tell me so far is that the body will be back in France by the end of this week and an announcement will be made then about a memorial service.'

'Do you think anyone in the family would talk to me about Philippe for a feature for the paper?' Daisy asked.

Bruno shook his head. 'Doubt it. The whole Cambone family appear to have closed ranks. They're not even talking to the French press.'

'Talk down at the Palais this afternoon was that there's some sort of scandal about to blow up,' Marcus said. 'That Mr Nice Guy Cambone wasn't all he seemed.'

Bruno glanced at him sharply. 'Philippe was the original Mr Nice Guy I can assure you.' Bruno sighed. 'Of course he's got this playboy reputation because he loved women — he was French after all. And women adored him. He stayed friends with his ex-lovers.'

Bruno stared into his champagne glass thoughtfully. 'Still can't believe he's gone.'

A loud burst of music drowned out his next remark and he smiled apologetically at Daisy. As the noise abated he handed her a business card.

'Nice to meet you. Ring me sometime if you want to talk about Philippe,' and he

51

turned to greet another guest.

Daisy looked around the crowded room trying to see if she recognized anyone famous. Unlike Poppy she did read the gossip magazines, purely in the name of research of course, and knew the faces of most of the 'A list' celebrities.

'Just spotted an old mate over by the bar,' Marcus shouted in her ear. 'Didn't expect to see him down here this year, he's had a few problems. Come and meet him,' and catching hold of her hand he led her across the room.

As Marcus tapped a tall man on his shoulder saying, 'Nat, how you doing?' Daisy recognized him. Cindy's minder.

They both smiled at each. 'You!' they said in unison.

'You two know each other?' Marcus asked.

'We've just seen each other around,' Nat said.

'Sorted your problem yet?' Marcus asked.

Nat shook his head. 'Still working on it. Hope to get it sorted during the festival.'

Marcus turned to Daisy. 'This guy is a brilliant writer but insists on working as a nanny.'

'A fellow's got to eat,' Nat protested, smiling at Daisy. 'And while the rogues in this business insist on pinching my ideas,' he shrugged. 'At least I've got a roof over my head. Besides, I like children. Now, if you'll excuse me I'm hoping there's a taxi waiting for me downstairs. I'll see you around.'

Impulsively Daisy said, 'I'm staying in the same direction as you — could I share your taxi?'

'Sure,' Nat replied easily.

Daisy looked at Marcus apologetically. 'I'm sorry but I am about to drop from exhaustion.'

Marcus placed a kiss on her cheek. 'Go home. I'll ring you tomorrow.'

Daisy looked at him. Now, why had he done that? Still being French or trying to stake a claim?

'I'll see her home safely for you, Marcus,' Nat said.

Daisy bit her lip. Nat had obviously got the idea from the kiss that she and Marcus were an item. Was that deliberate on Marcus's part?

The taxi was waiting when they got downstairs and Nat held the door open for Daisy before climbing in himself.

'Where are you staying?'

Daisy gave him the address and took a ten euro note out of her bag and offered it to Nat who shook his head. 'Don't worry about it. It's almost on my doorstep.'

'Thanks,' Daisy said. 'The little girl you're looking after, Cindy?' she said. 'Are her parents famous?'

'Verity Raymond and Teddy Wickham the director.'

'Verity Raymond as in actress?'

Nat nodded. 'Cindy's a sweet kid. Bit lonely at the moment. Misses her friends. But at least her father is here now. She adores him.'

'Maybe she'd like to meet up with Tom my nephew? They're about the same age.'

'That's a great idea. You and I could have a coffee together then? Look here's my number, give me a ring. I guess it will be easier for me to fit in a time around you as you're here to report on the festival.'

Daisy put the card Nat handed her in her bag. 'I'll find out what Tom is up to over the next few days and give you a ring,' she promised. 'Many thanks for the lift home.'

Cleaning her teeth before collapsing into bed, Daisy thought about Bruno's remarks regarding Philippe Cambone. If he was such a nice guy, why were there rumours starting to fly about him? Switching off the bedside light and snuggling down under the duvet though, it was thoughts of Nat and his blue eyes that filled her mind before she slept.

CHAPTER 4

Ten o'clock in the morning and Anna had found her way to her company's temporary office in one of the large hotels on the Croisette.

'OK Anna, I've made a hair appointment, here with Gaspard, for you,' the company's PR girl said, handing Anna an embossed business card.

'And the limo will collect you and Leo at seven o'clock to take you to the Palais des Festivals and again afterwards to take you down to the Palm Beach for the Party.

'There's also a couple of invitations here for various parties.'

The publicist glanced at Anna. 'I know you said you didn't really want to get involved with the party scene on your own, but this one in particular tomorrow night sounds fun. It's up in Super Californie in one of the big villas there.'

Anna hesitated and glanced across at Rick

her business partner and office manager. As always he was in total charge of things for Cannes week. She knew he'd been surprised when she'd told him she was coming to Cannes this year.

The deal had always been, Anna didn't do Cannes. A couple of the other festivals yes, but Rick was on his own for Cannes. He'd never asked why; just accepted it as a perk that he got to spend nearly a fortnight in the South of France every year. The networking he did was invaluable to the business and Anna had no intention of cramping his style in that regard.

'Usually a good evening,' he said now. 'The Americans attend this one in full force. There will be several people there who would love to meet you, including the eccentric Rosa Crufts.'

'Aren't we having dinner with her one day next week?'

Rick nodded. 'Yes, but an informal meet up at the party will break the ice. We can go together if you like,' he offered. 'Pick you up at nine o'clock.'

'Thanks,' Anna said, glancing at him. 'Rick, did you ever have any contact with Philippe Cambone down here?'

Rick shook his head. 'Shared a couple of cocktails with him at various parties down the years but that's about it. Different ends of the business so we were never going to be in regular contact. Seemed a nice bloke. Did hear on the grapevine that he was looking to cut back on work. Wanted to spend more time down here with his family and on his boat. Shame he didn't manage it. Why?'

'No reason, just that somebody at the villa I've rented asked if I'd ever worked with him and could I pass on any anecdotes for a feature she was writing.'

Rick shrugged. 'Sorry can't help. Right, I'm off to the Palais Stephanie for a meeting.'

'I'll walk down with you,' Anna said. 'I thought I'd have a mooch around Cannes this morning before going back to the villa. I need to find a supermarché too.'

At the hotel exit they went their separate ways.

'See you tomorrow evening,' Rick said before disappearing into the crowd, leaving Anna to cross the road and wander along the Croisette in the direction of the Palais des Festivals, soaking up the atmosphere.

Flags fluttering in the light breeze, huge billboards, pictures of Che Guevara everywhere, police dogs and their handlers creating wide paths before them as the slow-moving crowd parted to let them through, before surging back to close ranks again behind them. Buskers, clowns, starlets hoping to be discovered, locals out for some people watching and Philippino nannies bribing their young charges with ice cream as they gazed at the over the top glamour in the designer boutiques that lined the Croisette. Anna watched them all and marvelled.

Le Petit Train, still with a few vacant seats, was about to set off on its routine sightseeing trip around town and Anna wondered about hopping on board with the tourists. As she stood there undecided, the decision was made for her when the driver rang the bell and the train began to slowly manoeuvre its way through the crowds and traffic.

A small crowd had gathered around a middle-aged woman with startling hennared hair preparing to play an accordion. Anna, about to move on, found herself rooted to the spot as the woman began to sing Jézébel à la Edith Piaf.

With a voice eerily similar to that of the tragic star's, the modern day singer sent a frisson of déjà vu running through Anna's body. Once a favourite song of hers, she'd bought and played the record over and over again until, in a fit of blind rage the summer her world fell apart, she'd jumped on it and broken it into hundreds of pieces.

To hear that special song unexpectedly like this, in the place where the words had once been whispered so intimately to her, was heart-stoppingly hard. Anna turned and blindly followed a group of teenage would-be starlets crossing the road. As the girls made their way up a busy street towards the centre of town, Anna turned in the opposite direction and took a narrower, quieter street, away from the hurly-burly of the crowds.

A small park, a labyrinth of traffic free roads, and Anna slowly regained her composure. Another left turn and this street was busier, housing a florist, a fashion boutique, a couple of restaurants, the inevitable pharmacy and a tabac.

Anna sat at a pavement table at the smaller of the restaurants and ordered a coffee. Waiting for her drink to arrive she looked along the street with its tall narrow buildings, their window boxes overflowing with scarlet geraniums, blue shutters fastened against walls, excluding an air of tranquility absorbed down the centuries. A typical French street, it reminded Anna of countless others she'd seen before in towns up and down the country but there was something familiar about this particular street she couldn't place that was niggling at her.

'Merci,' she said as the waiter placed her demitasse coffee on the table before her. Sipping her drink she watched a couple of women, locals she guessed from their straw shopping baskets, talking animatedly together as they came out of the pharmacy. A few doors down, a well dressed woman was in earnest discussion with the florist before buying a large bunch of white lilies.

As the woman, carefully holding her flowers, walked purposefully past her, Anna wondered who the flowers were destined for. The woman crossed the road a few yards on and stopped outside a shuttered restaurant with a large 'Fermé' sign plastered across its door. Its pavement tables and chairs were piled up haphazardly, and there were numerous bunches of flowers already placed in the doorway.

Suddenly Anna realized where she was. Why the street seemed familiar. As the unknown woman placed the lilies in the shade of the doorway she didn't need to read the gold embossed name 'Chez Cambone' above the door to know it was Philippe's family restaurant; the flowers a tribute to him.

Her hand was shaking as she picked up her cup to take a steadying drink. Two reminders of her past on only her first day in Cannes. Was every day going to be like this? Her past forcing her to remember and wonder 'what if'?

'Are you home this evening?' Poppy asked as Daisy helped herself to a tumbler of water in the cottage kitchen late that afternoon. 'Or are you off partying again?'

Daisy shook her head. 'I've had enough for one day. I've got to finish writing up my daily report and send it, do a bit more to the Philippe Cambone feature — which reminds me. I must phone Marcus and see if he's got a photograph of the floral tributes that are apparently being laid at the door of the family restaurant, to send with my piece.' She took a drink before asking.

'Where's Tom?'

'Anna invited him over for a swim,' Poppy said. 'He'll be back soon.' She glanced at her sister. 'I've asked Anna to join us tonight. She seemed to be a bit low when I saw her this afternoon. Sad almost.'

'She doesn't seem to be getting involved in the festivities very much,' Daisy said thoughtfully. 'She must know people in the business that are down here but she did tell me doesn't like the limelight.'

'There's a big party tomorrow night apparently that she's thinking of going to. Anyway, I've asked her to join us for supper in the garden tonight,' Poppy said. 'No probing journalistic questions from you, mind,' she added, glancing at her sister sharply.

Daisy smiled. 'I promise. Now, when can Tom and Cindy get together? I told Nat I'd fix a time and ring him.'

'How about ice creams in the park tomorrow afternoon, see how they get on. Being the daughter of an actress, Cindy might be a bit precocious for Tom,' Poppy said. 'If they get on you can bring them back here for tea. Nat too.'

'Fine. I'll ring Nat,' Daisy said. 'Want me to help with supper?'

'No thanks,' Poppy said. 'It's just the usual quiche and stuff, cheese and baguettes. I'll get Tom to help me carry it out to the loggia table.' She looked at the kitchen clock. 'Think I'll go and fetch him — I'm sure Anna will have had enough of his chatter by now.'

'OK. I'll go and do my report and e-mail it. Might even find time to do some more research on Philippe Cambone,' Daisy said. 'See you in a bit.'

Anna swam another half dozen laps after

Poppy had collected Tom before getting out and going indoors for a shower. She was towelling her hair dry when Leo rang.

As always her heart lifted at the sound of his voice.

'Leo darling. How's your day been? Mine's been . . .' she hesitated, 'interesting.'

'Do I detect a note of distress?' Leo asked, the concern in his voice clear. 'Has something happened? Are you all right? I know Philippe's death was a shock to you.'

Anna sighed. 'No, nothing has happened to me other than a couple of memory-lane incidents that I'll tell you about when you get here.'

'Which will be a day early,' Leo said. 'One of my business meetings has been cancelled so I've rearranged my flight.'

'Oh Leo, that's wonderful.'

'Will you book a table for dinner somewhere? I hear there's a good place at Mougins.'

'I'll see what I can do,' Anna promised. 'I'm having supper with Poppy this evening, I'll ask her if there is anywhere special she can recommend.'

'Anna my darling, I've got to go. Alison wants my opinion on a cradle she's keen to buy — not that I really have any idea on such things. I'll ring you tomorrow. Love you.'

Anna smiled fondly at the thought of Alison and the expected baby. She could tell that Leo was already relishing his role of grandfather.

Half an hour later, taking a bottle of rosé out of the fridge, Anna made her way across the garden to the loggia attached to the cottage where Poppy had said they'd be eating supper.

Tom was busy putting cutlery and glasses on the gaily patterned Provençal tablecloth, before folding the matching napkins and placing them carefully on plates. Daisy was typing away on her laptop on a corner of the table and raised a hand in greeting as she mouthed 'Hi' in Anna's direction.

Poppy came out of the kitchen carrying bowls of salad and a quiche which she placed on the table. 'Hi — oh thanks,' as Anna handed her the bottle.

'Daisy will be finished soon and we'll eat. I must just light some candles before the midges decide to descend en masse. Grab a chair. I'll pour you a drink in a moment,' and Poppy took a match to several citronnelle candles that were dotted around.

Daisy closed the lid of her laptop with a flourish. 'Finished. Today's report sent and my piece about Philippe Cambone just needs the photo Marcus promised to take today.'

'Did you manage to uncover much information?' Anna asked curiously.

'Not a lot. But I did find a film biography site that mentioned his love of sailing so I put that in, and the fact that his twin brother still runs the family restaurant here in Cannes — not that he would talk to me. I decided not to mention the rumours that are floating around. Can always do another feature.'

'What rumours are those?' Anna asked, but before Daisy could answer, Poppy returned and the question was forgotten.

'Let's eat,' Poppy said, placing a bowl of buttered asparagus and new potatoes on the table. 'Bon appétit.'

'How are you enjoying the festival?' Daisy asked, looking at Anna. 'Have to say I'm already feeling exhausted at the sheer pace of things. Goodness knows how people actually in the trade cope with the frantic networking and partying that is going on.'

'Haven't really seen a great deal of it yet,' Anna replied. 'It's certainly different to the first time I was here.'

Daisy looked at her in surprise. 'I thought . . .'

Anna looked at her. 'I think I owe you an apology, Daisy. The trade-paper bio you read got it wrong.'

Anna swirled the wine in her glass reflectively before looking up and saying, 'I was here in '68, the year the festival was closed early. I was in my first year at Art College and had managed to get a job as a messenger for the duration of the festival for a small UK film company.' She smiled at Daisy.

'Unfortunately it didn't work out as planned. But then I've found life itself rarely does.'

'That's true,' Poppy said. 'I never expected to be living in France but here I am. May I give you some quiche, Anna?'

Anna held her plate out. 'Please. And you, Daisy? Is life working out for you so far?'

Daisy considered the question. 'Well, my love life hasn't lived up to expectations, that's for sure. I guess I'm lucky with my career going very much the way I wanted since I left university. I'm toying with the idea of going freelance though, so whether that will mess things up remains to be seen.'

'What sort of freelance writing?' Anna asked.

'Lifestyle features. Property. Anything but hard nosed reporting,' Daisy said. 'I'm finding it difficult to justify the kind of intrusive journalism that seems to be the norm these days. I guess I'm just not nosey enough; I think people are entitled to their privacy — unless they've done something criminally wrong of course and it needs exposing "in the public interest" as they say.'

She looked at Anna, 'How long did it take you to establish your business? Did you have lots of contacts before you went independent?'

'Oh it was years before I felt brave enough to go solo. Meeting Rick — my business partner — was the catalyst,' Anna said. 'With hindsight there are lots of things I would have done differently, but in general, I suppose my working life has turned out fine.'

She turned to Poppy. 'Talking of work, can you help me organize a party here at the villa next week? Or tell me where I can get help?'

'No problem,' Poppy answered. 'Glad to help. We'll get together in the next couple of days and work things out.'

'The other thing is, Leo wants me to book a table somewhere special for dinner on Saturday evening, any ideas? He mentioned somewhere in Mougins. Le Moulin something or other?'

Poppy pulled a face. 'Difficult. I suspect the place he means will already be fully booked. It's expensive and a favourite with the celebrities. Everywhere gets so busy this fortnight. You might have to go to Antibes or even Cagnes-sur-mer.'

'I can always do something here. I saw a couple of delicatessens with some mouth-watering food this morning,' Anna said. 'In fact I think I'll do that. Especially as it's the day before the premiere — I don't want a late night.'

Poppy stood up. 'Come on, Tom. Bedtime for you. Say goodnight. Daisy, help Anna to some more dessert.'

'How many people are you inviting for your party next week?' Daisy asked as she offered Anna the bowl of fruit salad and some meringues.

'Thirty — thirty-five. I doubt everyone will come. Depends on what else is on the same evening. These meringues are delicious.'

A loud croak from a frog somewhere in the garden made them both smile.

'Now that's something I remember from my first visit down here,' Anna said. 'There were a lot of croaking frogs. I was staying in a run down guest house with a stagnant pond in the overgrown garden; the noise was unbelievable.'

'It gets quite noisy in this garden too sometimes,' Daisy said absently. 'Anna, I've just had an idea. Would you talk to me about the differences you find in the festival this time around? The way it's developed from those early days? Maybe we could walk around Cannes together, a nostalgic walk for you, a history lesson for me.'

'Oh, Daisy, I don't know. I'm not sure that . . .' Anna shook her head, thinking about her memory lane incidents earlier in the day.

'Will you at least think about it?' Daisy asked. 'So much must have changed in the last forty years — not just buildings being pulled down and re-built but people's lives have altered too. You could always remain anonymous if you want, but I think the comparison between then and now would interest a lot of people.'

'I'm not sure I remember enough to highlight the differences,' Anna said slowly. 'I was barely seventeen. Of course I remember the atmosphere, the students and the old Palais des Festivals but —' Anna shook her head.

Poppy returned at that moment with a pot of coffee and Anna accepted a cup, glad to be able to change the subject.

'I meant to say earlier, you will both come to the party won't you?'

'Love to,' Daisy said, picking up her mobile from the table. 'Excuse me, I've got a text from Marcus — oh it's ok. It's just to tell me he's sent the photo for my feature and forwarded me a copy too.'

As the sonar garden lights flickered into action, Anna stood up to leave.

'Thank you both for a lovely evening. I was feeling a bit low this afternoon and you've really cheered me up. Can I help clear the table? No, you're sure?' as Poppy shook her head. 'I'll see you tomorrow then.'

'Don't forget to think about my feature idea will you?' Daisy asked, opening her laptop to check the photo Marcus had sent.

'Oh Daisy,' Anna said shaking her head. 'I'll think about it but I'm not promising to do it. Goodnight,' and Anna turned and began to make her way across the garden to the villa.

'Poppy, look at this,' Daisy said, turning her laptop around so Poppy could see the picture. 'Is that who I think it is about to place a single rose with the other tributes?'

'Think so,' Poppy said, looking at the screen intently. 'The soft focus has given it a certain ethereal look but yes, that's Anna.'

They both looked across the garden and

returned Anna's last goodnight wave as she disappeared into the villa.

'I wish I'd looked at this before she said goodnight,' Daisy said. 'I could have asked her why she was leaving a tribute to a man she said she'd never worked with — and presumably didn't know?'

'I thought you said earlier people were entitled to their privacy?' Poppy said. 'It's really none of our business.'

'True,' Daisy said. 'But I can't help wondering all the same.'

CHAPTER 5

Daisy was up early the next morning and walked down to Cannes for an early screening and the following press conference. Afterwards she made her way across to one of the many cafés on the square and ordered a couple of croissants to go with her coffee.

She was sitting there eavesdropping on the conversations going on around her and trying to get some coherent thoughts about the film she'd just seen on to her laptop when Marcus briefly kissed her cheek and sat down beside her. She really was going to have to have a word about all this kissing.

'Hi. How's it going?'

'Fine. You? Caught any celebrities in flagrante?' Daisy asked.

Marcus shook his head. 'Not yet but I live in hope. Uncovered any interesting titbits for Bill?'

'No. Thanks for the photo by the way. Was

72

Anna alone? Did you speak to her?' Daisy asked.

'Anna?'

'The woman in the photograph.'

'Didn't see anyone else. And no, I didn't speak to her,' Marcus said slowly. 'I'm surprised you recognized the woman. I deliberately went for a slight out of focus shot because I wanted the poignancy of a mourner laying a tribute without identification. Who is she, anyway?'

'She runs a production company and has rented the villa for the festival,' Daisy said. 'She's a nice lady, but,' Daisy hesitated. 'Very private,' she said finally, wondering how Anna would react if she ever saw the photograph.

'You talked to her about Cambone?'

'I tried. She's not very forthcoming about him. Says she never worked with him,' Daisy said. 'But she must have known him surely to lay a tribute flower.'

Marcus yawned. 'Sorry. Didn't get to bed until three this morning. See if you can get her to open up a bit more. Whatever Bruno says, there is something bubbling behind the Cambone family's silence. The fact they won't talk to anyone is suspicious.'

'They might just want their privacy at a sad time?' Daisy suggested tentatively.

Marcus shrugged. 'Privacy is rarely an option in the film business. Right, I'm off to take some pics of the celebs on the beach. You want to come too?'

'No thanks. I'm going to have a wander around, see if I can pick up some gossip in the shopping mall before I have lunch with a PR from one of the film agencies. Thought I might take a look at the floral tributes too,' Daisy said.

The windows of the shopping mall that linked the Croisette with the rue d'Antibes were filled with expensive clothes, jewellery and the latest must-have handbags. As Daisy wandered around, advertising flyer after flyer was pressed into her hand by young girls and boys keen to publicize their talents and catch the eye of anybody who could turn them into the stars they dreamed of being. Daisy stuffed the flyers into her bag. She'd look at them later — there might be an interesting story in there somewhere.

A couple were entertaining the crowd with a juggling act. Near the mall exit doorway a violinist was setting up his music as the gendarmes moved a couple of beggars and their dogs on. Outside, the streets in the centre of town were teeming with hawkers, buskers and human statues. It was all very colourful and noisy.

It took Daisy nearly ten minutes to reach Chez Cambone after leaving the mall. Although still firmly closed to customers, she saw the flowers had been moved to one side allowing access through the restaurant door.

Slowly Daisy began to read the tributes as she looked for the single rose she knew Anna had placed in the doorway. 'A sad loss', 'One of the greats', 'You'll be missed'.

There were two single roses — both red and both with attached cards.

'Good-bye and God bless' read one. The other: 'One Life. One Love. Farewell'. Neither bore a signature.

As Daisy stood there holding them, wondering which rose Anna had placed there, which inscription was from her, the restaurant door opened. Bruno came out accompanied by another man who Daisy guessed was Jacques Cambone, Philippe's twin brother.

The two men shook hands and Jacques disappeared back indoors, closing the door firmly behind him, without acknowledging Daisy's presence.

'Hi,' Bruno said. 'Sorry, don't think Jacques was in the mood to be introduced. I've finally got some dates out of him for the funeral and the memorial service. The funeral will be on Monday — strictly private and no details will be issued to the public.'

'Are you going?' Daisy asked.

Bruno nodded. 'Of course. I'm doing a reading. Hoping my son will be able to get here in time too.'

'The memorial service?' Daisy asked.

'The following Monday morning, open to everyone.'

'The buzz at the press conference this morning was that an Irish actor called Sean Hamill is somehow involved in a scandal involving Philippe Cambone,' Daisy said, watching for Bruno's reaction.

He shrugged. 'We'll see. The Cambones have got the police looking into him. But — and this is not for publicizing yet — if it becomes general knowledge too soon, I'll know who to blame as, so far, I'm the only person outside the Cambone family who knows what I am about to tell you.' Bruno paused before continuing. 'Two letters have been found amongst Philippe's effects from someone trying to trace their family tree.'

'Is this why the Cambones have closed ranks? Worried about losing his money to a stranger?'

Bruno nodded.

'Are these letters from this Sean Hamill?' Daisy asked.

'I don't know,' Bruno shrugged. 'I didn't get to read the letters and Jacques was being pretty coy about their contents. He certainly didn't name names. But it was pretty clear that Philippe had replied to the first letter. The second one arrived in response to it the day Philippe died.'

Bruno looked at the flowers Daisy was still holding. 'From you?'

'Oh. No,' Daisy said. 'I was just reading the messages. This one has a certain regretful solicitous tone to it.'

Bruno, bending down to read some of the other messages straightened up. 'Why? What does it say?'

'One Life, One Love. Farewell.'

'Show me the card,' Bruno said, holding his hand out. 'Is it signed?'

Bruno took a deep breath as he looked at the card with its message. 'One Life. One Love,' he muttered under his breath, before looking at Daisy.

'I'd bet the Palme d'Or on the fact that this Sean Hamill didn't write the letters, or that he has any connection to Philippe,' he said, thoughtfully fingering the card.

'But this — this is different — a real link to the past. Philippe used this phrase a lot at a certain stage of his life. Whoever wrote this knew Philippe Cambone intimately.'

■ ■ ■ ■

From her table at the Carlton Beach Restaurant, Anna had a clear view of the numerous luxury yachts moored out in the bay. In the distance the Isle of Saint-Marguerite lay serene in the midday sun, the Mediterranean gently lapping at its sandy shores. Noise from the helicopters busily ferrying VIPs to the Palm Beach complex at the far eastern end of the Croisette, added to the hubbub of sounds all around.

Anna reached for her tumbler of water. Lunch had been delicious — tuna salade niçoise followed by a mouth watering glacé with summer fruits and mascarpone. Reneé Porteous, the Parisian who represented the company in France, had been full of enthusiasm for the coming year. Now she'd left for another meeting, Anna and Rick were sitting there mulling over the things that had been discussed and taking in the atmosphere.

All around life, as one big social networking event, was busy: People talking animatedly on their mobiles, men in Armani suits and actresses dressed to seduce, air kissed; ladies who lunched with coiffeured hair and their inevitable toy dogs, were busy seeing and being seen. Two policemen, arms folded across their chests, were standing regarding the diners thoughtfully.

'Wonder who or what they're after,' Rick said, as one of the policemen, his gun visibly protruding from his waist holster, began to weave his way between the tables towards a large group of diners. Judging by the noise they were making and the number of empty bottles on the table, the party had clearly indulged themselves over lunch.

Turning her head to look, Anna felt her heart lurch in her chest. Sitting three tables away was Jacques Cambone. For a fraction of a second Anna believed it was Philippe — the likeness was so startling. Both Jacques and the man he was lunching with, were watching the police intently. There was something vaguely familiar about the other man, but Anna couldn't quite place him.

The rowdy table had fallen silent as the policeman approached. A fair-haired man, clearly the subject of the policeman's interest, had pushed his chair back and was standing up.

'Yeah. Sure. I'm Sean Hamill,' Anna heard him say in a drunken drawl. 'What's the problem?'

The policeman's reply was lost in the general buzz as he reached in a pocket for a pair of handcuffs, which he proceeded to snap around Sean Hamill's wrists, before indicating with a jerk of his head and a pull of his arm, he was to accompany him.

'Hey lighten up, man. It was just a publicity stunt. A joke.'

As Sean and the policemen passed their table, Anna and Rick got a good look at him. Late thirties, tall, sunglasses pushed up into his fashionably long hair, expensive loafers on his feet, wearing white jeans and polo shirt, he appeared unfazed by his arrest.

'Interesting,' Rick said. 'That's the actor who's been claiming to be related to Philippe Cambone.'

Shocked, Anna looked at him before slowly turning and looked at Jacques in time to see him glance at his companion and mutter 'Good. Hopefully that should put a stop to it.'

'Right,' Rick said, pushing his chair back and standing. 'I'm off. See you this evening. The party,' he added as Anna looked at him puzzled. 'Super Californie?'

'Sorry, I'd completely forgotten,' Anna answered. 'See you later then.'

Anna sat for a few moments after Rick had left, lost in her thoughts. She turned to look at Jacques and his companion. Idly she found herself wondering how Jacques would react if she approached him to offer her condolences about Philippe. Would he recognize her or simply accept her platitudes about his brother as coming from an ex-colleague? Would he introduce her to his friend?

One of the African beach sellers approached, offering a selection of watches and sunglasses, kaftans and various other items. Anna shook her head, the interruption breaking her thoughts.

'Non merci,' and the man continued his hopeful trawl around the restaurant tables.

Reflectfully she looked out across the bay towards the islands — was life over there still as simple and idyllic as it had appeared to be, forty years ago?

If there was time, she'd suggest she and Leo take one of the local ferry boats and spend a couple of hours wandering around Saint-Marguerite. She knew Leo would be intrigued by the story of the Man in the Iron Mask who'd been held captive for decades in the ancient fort there.

Jacques Cambone and his friend had stood up and were walking towards her table on their way to the beach exit. Anna felt a jolt of recognition as she saw the face of Jacques' companion. She couldn't remember his name but she was certain it was a friend of Philippe's whom she'd met years ago. She half stood up to speak to him, to claim acquaintance, to offer Jacques her condolences, but sank back down again on to her chair without speaking. What was the point? It couldn't possibly serve any purpose, so was best left.

CHAPTER 6

'What did you mean about the rogues in this business the other day?' Daisy asked Nat as they stood on the Croisette, watching Tom and Cindy on the carousel.

'Somebody, pretending to be interested in representing me, took my last script and got it commissioned as his own work,' Nat said ruefully.

'That's awful,' Daisy said. 'Couldn't you expose him?'

Nat shook his head. 'Unfortunately there's no copyright in ideas and he'd altered the script just enough to make it difficult for me to prove anything. So from now on I intend to be more careful whom I trust and make sure I register everything with the script-writers' union and other places.'

'Did it become a big film?'

Nat nodded. 'Oh yes. It did very well at the box office — I wouldn't have had any money problems for years. C'est la vie,' and shrugging his shoulders, he smiled at Daisy.

'Can't Teddy Wickham help you get started? He must know all sorts of people in the business,' Daisy said, waving to Tom and Cindy as they passed by, each sitting on a gaily painted carousel horse.

'He's promised to introduce me to a couple of producers this week,' Nat answered, 'but being on the jury he's very busy. It's Cindy's birthday next week too. He's hoping to be able to at least spend a couple of hours with her that day.'

'Is Verity planning anything special?'

'Lots of presents and treats here, and then a big party when they get back home.'

As the carousel glided to a stop, Daisy and Nat helped the two children off.

'Time for ice creams now,' Daisy said. 'And then back to the cottage for tea.'

Poppy was sitting at the kitchen table writing a long list when they got home.

'Hi. Tea will be in ten minutes. Tom, why don't you show Cindy your tree house — but stay away from the villa. Anna's just gone for a siesta by the pool. Try not to disturb her.'

Daisy glanced at the list. 'You and Anna sorted things?'

'Yes. She wants a "1920s on the Cote d'Azur" theme. She's asked me to try and find a pianist for the night — thank goodness I had the piano tuned last month!'

'Sounds fun,' Daisy said. 'As guests, do we get to wear flapper dresses? I've forgotten — which evening is it? Must make sure I'm not busy.'

'Tuesday. Don't know about flapper dresses — I'm going to be in a bit of a flap I think. Can you help me with things? It's a bigger event than I thought it was going to be.' Poppy appealed to her sister. 'I'm beginning to wish I hadn't offered to do the catering.'

'Tom can come and play with Cindy after school for a couple of hours Monday and Tuesday, if that's any help,' Nat said. 'They seem to be getting on well,' he added, as a burst of childish laughter drifted across the garden from the tree house.

'That would be brilliant, thanks,' Poppy answered. 'Now all I need to do is work my way through this list before next week.'

'Don't worry, sis, it'll all work out,' Daisy said reassuringly. 'Right now though, you'd better get some tea organized for Tom and Cindy before Nat has to take Cindy home and I have to get back down to Cannes. Eating outside? I'll lay the table and then go and get the children.'

Walking out into the garden Daisy saw

Anna, asleep on a sunbed under one of the pool-side parasols. Tom waved from the tree house and Daisy beckoned to them to come down, before turning to go back to the cottage.

As they tiptoed past the end of the swimming pool, Tom told Cindy in a loud stage whisper, 'That's my friend Anna. She's really nice. She lets me swim in the pool with her. She's come for the festival like your mum and dad.'

'Is she a film star like Mummy?' Cindy whispered back.

'Gosh no,' Tom said. 'She's too old. I think she helps make the films.'

Anna opened her eyes. 'Hello Tom. Who's this?'

'This is my new friend Cindy. Her mummy is an actress.'

'Hello Cindy,' Anna said. 'That's a pretty name.'

'It's really Lucinda,' Cindy said. 'My mummy wanted me to be Charlotte but Daddy really wanted Lucinda, so Mummy said yes. My full name is Lucinda Charlotte Natasha,' and Cindy smiled at Anna.

Anna sat up and looked at Cindy.

'And is your daddy an actor too?'

Cindy shook her head. 'No. I don't know what he does but he's always very busy,' she said seriously. 'It's my birthday next week,' she said. 'Mummy says we might go and see the whales but Daddy doesn't know yet if he can come.'

'And how old will you be?' Anna asked.

'Six.'

'Tom. Cindy. Teatime. Leave Anna in peace,' Poppy called.

'Bye Anna,' Tom and Cindy said together as they ran over to the cottage.

Anna pushed her sunglasses to the top of her head and watched the children disappearing into the cottage, before slowly making her way into the villa to prepare for the party in Super Californie she'd promised to attend with Rick.

With Cindy between them holding their hands, Daisy and Nat walked down to the grand belle époque villa where Teddy Wickham and his family were staying for the Festival. Nat pressed the security button, the gate swung open and Cindy skipped inside. Nat glanced at Daisy.

'I've got tickets for the cinema on the beach tomorrow evening, want to join me? Not sure what's showing — could be Tom and Jerry or a decent classic feature.'

'Hey, don't knock Tom and Jerry,' Daisy laughed. 'I'm a big fan. Shall I see you by the Carlton beach after the evening's red carpet proceedings? I'll need to take a look at that first. Should be finished about eight o'clock.'

'Look forward to it. Thanks for this afternoon,' and Nat followed Cindy into the landscaped villa gardens.

As Daisy cut through the back streets of Cannes and made her way down to the old port, she thought about Nat. How nice he was. How kind he was. How different he was to Ben. And those blue eyes of his were . . . were spellbinding, she decided. It would be fun getting to know him better.

Several of the yachts moored alongside the quay were hosting parties and Daisy caught snippets of conversations in French, Italian and what she took to be Russian as she walked past a white hulled sailing yacht where a television crew were on board busily filming a bikini clad actress.

Dodging the crowds that were still swarming around the tents of the Village International, Daisy made her way to the front of the Palais des Festivals hoping to find Marcus there. He might have heard some more gossip regarding the rumours that were circulating about Philippe Cambone.

There was the usual scrum of paparazzi that Daisy had come to expect hanging around the red carpet entrance to the Palais. It was several moments before she finally spotted Marcus busy snapping a blonde girl getting into a red Ferrari parked near the red carpet.

'You get my text?' he asked turning to greet Daisy, as the Ferrari engine revved noisily before taking off down the Croisette with its passenger, at an enforced sedate pace. 'Dinner tomorrow night?'

Daisy shook her head. 'Sorry. Nat's already asked me to go to the beach cinema with him.'

'Okay. We'll make it next Tuesday evening.' Marcus sighed when Daisy shook her head again.

'It's Anna's party at the villa and I've been invited.'

'Can I come?'

'I'll ask Anna,' Daisy promised. 'We could have that dinner Bill is treating us to, this evening if you like?' she suggested tentatively. 'I'm not dressed for anywhere too posh but —'

'Bruno's got me an invite to a swish party,' Marcus interrupted. 'In fact it's time I showered and got into my evening suit. I'll see you around,' and he was gone.

Pensively Daisy crossed the Croisette. Surely Marcus could have wangled an invite for her too? Daisy wandered slowly along looking at the expensive boutiques. It was impossible to see much because of the crowds and in the end she gave up and made for a seat under a palm tree in the nearby gardens of the Hotel de Ville. Fishing in her bag she found her tape recorder and quietly started to record some notes for her next report.

'As the sun sets, flashing lights and neon signs take over in the twilight, indicating that the glamorous nightlife of Cannes, which will continue into the early hours, is once again starting. The "Welcome to the Cannes Film Festival" illuminated sign strung across the road reminds you, in case you forget, you're on the Cote d'Azur at the world famous event. Out in the bay I can see lights on Roberto Cavalli's large purple yacht where the crew are preparing for a big party on board; among other celebrities, Naomi Campbell is rumoured to be a guest.

'Limousines are beginning to discharge their VIP passengers at the foot of the Palais steps to face a barrage of flashlights and shouts of admiration from the waiting crowds. Fans push each other aside in a desperate attempt to obtain the autograph of their favourite star.

'Music is pounding from cars as they

move slowly along the Croisette, under the censorious gaze of stern-faced gendarmes. The weather tonight is perfect for the cinema on the beach. People are hurrying past me to claim a seat on the sand under the stars, ready to watch a movie in a truly romantic setting with the Mediterranean gently lapping at the shoreline and a balmy breeze providing the best air conditioning.'

Daisy switched off the recorder, slipped it back into her bag and sat for a few moments people watching before getting up and walking back to the villa.

Poppy was sitting reading under the loggia. 'Wasn't expecting you until later. Everything all right? Wine's in the fridge.'

'I guess it's busy down town?' she added.

'Mayhem. Poppy, can we talk? I had a letter from Ben before I flew out here.'

Poppy closed her book. 'And? What did he say?'

Daisy took the letter out of her bag and handed it to her sister. 'Read it. I'm going to have a shower.'

A bottle of wine, glasses and a plate of sliced baguette and jambon with melon was on the table when she returned. 'Honestly Poppy, I'm going to be so fat by the end of the festival. Everything seems to revolve around drink and food down here.'

'Because it's France. It's the way they are — besides, food helps me concentrate,' Poppy said, helping herself to a slice of melon. 'So what are you going to do about Ben? Are you going to fly halfway around the world and run back into his arms as he suggests?'

'Don't know,' Daisy said pouring two glasses of wine. 'Was hoping you'd help me decide.' When Poppy didn't answer she continued. 'Part of me thinks no but then another part says yes.'

'Big decision. I know he says he misses you and "thinks" he's made a mistake but really Daisy, he could just be homesick. You could pack everything in at home, get out there and find it's you who's made the mistake.'

Daisy nodded. 'I know.' She took a sip of wine. 'I could go for a holiday, say three weeks. I'd surely know by the end of it whether I wanted to stay or not. Wouldn't I?'

'How much do you really miss Ben these days? And I mean, really miss? You said you were enjoying being single.'

'I am. But you know how it is. It's nice to have someone special in your life. Someone who really cares.'

'Which Ben clearly didn't, otherwise he

wouldn't have buggered off to Australia in the first place, would he?' Poppy demanded.

Daisy looked at her sister. Poppy so rarely swore she knew the whole idea of her sister jetting off to Australia and taking up with Ben again had upset her.

'Only you can decide, Daisy,' Poppy said. 'But personally I think you'd be making a huge mistake in running after Ben. Unless of course it's true love on both your parts. And I have to say, I somehow doubt that.'

CHAPTER 7

Anna put the finishing touches to her makeup before making her way downstairs to wait for Rick and the taxi. She was already regretting agreeing to go to this party; these events were simply not her scene but she supposed it was too late to back out now. She glanced at her watch. Just time to give Leo a quick ring before she left.

'Not sure what time I'll get back here from this party,' she said when he answered. 'So I thought I'd ring you first. How are you? And Alison?'

'Everything is fine this end. Can't wait for tomorrow,' Leo answered. 'Hope to be with you about four. Have you booked us somewhere nice for dinner?

Before Anna could tell him her plans, a car horn sounded outside the villa.

'Got to go. Rick's here early. Love you. See you tomorrow.'

The taxi took Anna and Rick quickly up through town and into the affluent area of Super Californie where they caught glimpses of imposing villas hidden away behind large iron gates and towering cypress hedges.

'Have we had many acceptances yet for our party on Tuesday?' Anna asked.

'Twenty definites, eight refusals so far and fifteen still to answer,' Rick said.

'So we'll probably end up with about forty people?' Anna said thoughtfully. 'Including us, Leo, Daisy and Poppy.'

The taxi slowed and joined a queue of vehicles edging their way between open intricate wrought iron gates on to a gravelled driveway that finally stopped in front of an impressive flight of steps leading to a grand column-dominated entrance.

'This place is something else isn't it?' Rick said as they walked into the huge marbled entrance hall, with its four overhead chandeliers casting their palatial glow over everything.

An elaborately carved four foot high gold fountain, decorated with naked nymphs and grapes, was gently tinkling water into its two basins, from where it flowed over into a marble lined base where goldfish could be seen swimming under water lily leaves.

Liveried footmen holding silver trays full of crystal flutes filled with pink champagne moved effortlessly through the crowd, dispensing the drinks. Rick took two, handed one to Anna and said, 'Cheers.'

'Cheers,' Anna replied, looking around at the paintings and tapestries hanging on the walls under elaborate gold friezes.

'I've been in some luxurious places,' she said. 'But this is amazing. Are those original Picassos and Renoirs? Who does this place belong to?'

Rick shrugged. 'Some Arab prince or other. The main event is in the marquee on the terrace. Shall we?'

Anna followed him as he made his way out through open French doors leading on to the terrace and acres of landscaped gardens.

'Just spotted Rosa Cruft. Come on, I'll introduce you,' Rick said.

Rosa, talking animatedly to a man who had his back to them as they approached, smiled in welcome.

'Hi there Ricky. Great to meet you at last, Anna. You guys know Bruno?'

As the American made the introductions and Bruno shook her hand, Anna found herself face to face with the man she'd seen earlier in the day with Jacques Cambone.

'Anna? Haven't we've met before? Are you in the business?'

Anna didn't answer his first question, saying 'Yes I am in the film industry. Rick and I are business partners. You?'

'I'm in finance. You sure we haven't met? Something very familiar about your face. We must get together sometime and discuss our pasts,' Bruno said, smiling at her.

'Maybe,' Anna said lightly, before turning to face Rosa.

'Rosa, I'm looking forward to our lunch next week. Now, if you will excuse me, I need to find the cloakroom. Back in a few moments,' and Anna made her way back into the mansion.

One of the liveried footmen pointed her in the direction of the ladies' cloakroom. To her relief it was empty and Anna stood in front of the large gilded mirror above a marble sink with gold taps and tried to re-apply her lipstick with a shaking hand. She'd finally remembered who Bruno was.

So why hadn't she admitted to him that yes he did indeed know her? That he had known her when she was with Philippe. Because in those days he had been plain Brian, Philippe's best friend, and she wasn't sure what his reaction would be when he learnt her true identity.

She glanced at her watch. How soon before she could decently leave? Quarter of an hour? Or longer? She sighed before resolutely returning to the marquee and regarding the party scene.

Disco music with a loud beat was filling the air and people were dancing. Anna saw Rick and Rosa Cruft in the middle of a large crowd to one side of the tent. Bruno was listening attentively to something a younger man at his side, his arm around the shoulders of a blonde girl, was saying.

As she watched, Bruno turned his head and looked directly at her and Anna knew that he had finally recognized her. Following his gaze the other man too turned and looked across at her, before leaning and muttering something to Bruno.

Smiling, Bruno slowly raised his arm in greeting and beckoned her to join them. In a daze, Anna acknowledged the greeting before turning away to make for the exit. To her relief a doorman was able to immediately summon her a taxi and she sank down gratefully on to its upholstered seats. She would go home and dream about Leo and her future — not dwell on the past.

Anna was having a leisurely breakfast on the terrace the next morning when her mobile rang. Rick.

'How are you this morning?' he asked.

'Fine. I'm sorry I ran out on you last night,' Anna said apologetically.

'Not a problem,' Rick answered. 'I know those sort of do's aren't your thing. Anyway, it's not what I'm ringing about. Thing is, a courier has just arrived here with a package for you marked 'Private and Confidential'. Shall I send him up to the villa or do you want to come into the office and collect it?'

'Any idea who it's from?' Anna asked.

'No. There isn't a company name or anything on the envelope. It is marked urgent though.'

'You'd better send it up here then,' Anna said. 'I hadn't planned on coming down to the office today. Thanks.'

By the time the motorbike courier arrived fifteen minutes later, Anna had given up trying to second guess who the package was from and what it contained.

Wandering back into the villa, she stood in the sitting room examining the envelope for clues before slowly opening it. Inside, a sheet of writing paper was folded around a photocopy of a black and white photograph.

Two young people, arms entwined around each other smiled happily at the camera. Anna bit her lip, recognizing herself and

Philippe in the photograph. In the white space at the bottom Anna could just read the words that had been scrawled across the bottom of the original photograph: 'One Life. One Love.'

Standing there holding the old photograph of herself and Philippe, Anna felt all the emotions of her teenage love flooding through her body. She remembered being so happy the evening this photograph was taken.

They'd taken a boat across to Saint-Marguerite with a group of Philippe's friends and spent the day lazing on the beach and swimming. She and Philippe had slipped away from the group for an hour or two and Philippe had taken her to see an empty cottage with wonderful views across the bay.

'It belongs to my family,' he said. 'I shall restore it and we will live the simple life here,' he'd said. 'Our children will have a childhood to remember.'

Laughingly Anna had protested, 'We've only known each other three days and you've already got us married.'

Philippe had taken her in his arms then. 'But already, I know you're the only one for me. I want to spend the rest of my life making love to you.'

A barbecue on the beach later that evening had been the perfect end to a wonderful day for Anna. As they sat side by side in the boat on the return journey, Philippe, his arm around her shoulders holding her tight, had whispered again and again, 'Je t'aime. I love you,' and Anna had thought she would explode with happiness.

Now, as she stared blurry-eyed at the photograph, the question was, who had sent her the print?

Apprehensively as the tears finally began to flow down her cheeks, Anna unfolded the writing paper and read the message it contained.

'Please, I beg you, have lunch with me today — 1 p.m. The Auberge, Cannes. I need to talk to you about Philippe Cambone.' The message was signed simply, 'Bruno'.

Sinking down on to the settee, Anna gazed unseeingly out of the window, questions spinning around in her head. How had Bruno come by the photo?

Thoughtfully Anna brushed the tears away. She'd come to Cannes this year determined to talk to Philippe Camborne and put the past to rest, only to have his unexpected death put paid to her plans in that respect. Could Bruno answer some of the questions she'd planned to ask Philippe? Could she talk to him as she'd planned to talk with Philippe?

Resolutely she stood up. She would have lunch with Bruno and listen to what he had to say. Then when Leo got here that afternoon, she'd talk to him truthfully about the past and they would decide together how to deal with it as she finally put it behind her.

Picking up the phone, she booked a taxi to collect her at quarter to one. She'd spend the rest of the morning swimming and relaxing by the pool, and try not to think about the past too much.

Anna dressed carefully for her lunch appointment with Bruno, and was ready and waiting when the taxi arrived. Fighting a sudden inclination to tell the driver to go away, she'd changed her mind and didn't need a taxi, she climbed into the back and hoped he knew where The Auberge was.

The streets were busy with the midday rush hour traffic and Anna was five minutes late arriving at the restaurant in a quiet back street. The maitre d'hôtel came forward to greet her as the doorman ushered her in.

'Mon ami, Monsieur . . .' she started to say before realizing she didn't know Bruno's last name.

Anna hesitated, looking around her hoping to spot Bruno.

The maitre d' glanced at a list of reservations, 'Madame Carson?'

When Anna nodded, he said, 'This way, s'il vous plaît,' and he led Anna through the full restaurant out into a wisteria covered courtyard where Bruno was waiting for her at a secluded table in the corner.

'I'm sorry I'm late,' Anna apologized. 'I'd forgotten how busy the traffic is at this time of day.'

'I was afraid you'd decided against coming,' Bruno said.

'I almost did,' Anna confessed. 'I don't normally accept lunch invitations from,' she hesitated. 'Strangers.'

'But I'm not a complete stranger,' Bruno said. 'I'm an old acquaintance you lost touch with. Shall we order?'

Anna took the menu from the waiter. 'I'm not really hungry. I'll just have a salad.' She glanced sharply at Bruno, who sighed.

'Anna, this is one of the finest restaurants in town, it would be a crime not to enjoy your meal here. So order something you like then, if we fall out and never speak to each other again, at least you will have had an enjoyable meal to remember.'

In spite of herself Anna smiled. 'Okay. Do you recommend anything in particular?'

'For starters I'm going to have roasted figs with goat's cheese, followed by the sea bass baked in a salt crust. If I've got any room left I shall then indulge in the chef's splendid chocolate truffle cake.'

'Sounds delicious — I'll have the same,' Anna said.

'In which case I'll order us a bottle of white wine,' Bruno said.

As the wine waiter uncorked Bruno's choice and offered it for his inspection, Anna studied Bruno. Was he really the person she'd known as Brian? Watching him as he lifted the glass to his lips to taste the wine, she noticed the middle finger of his left hand was a deformed stump. The confirmation she needed.

Bruno nodded at the wine waiter, waited as he filled both glasses before raising his and saying softly, 'Here's to Philippe. Rest in peace.'

Silently Anna held her glass aloft in acknowledgement and took a sip, before saying quietly, 'You're Brian, aren't you?'

He nodded.

'You know who I am?' she said putting her glass on the table.

'Yes. The love of Philippe's life.'

'I'm surprised you recognized me after all these years.'

'I didn't totally at first,' Bruno said. 'There was just something about your face that seemed hauntingly familiar. It wasn't until a photographer friend last evening told me he'd seen you placing a flower in tribute to Philippe, that the truth dawned on me.'

He glanced at her. 'I'd seen the message "One Life. One Love" with the flower and knew you'd finally returned — albeit too late for Philippe to know.'

He regarded her over the rim of his glass and took a sip before saying, 'But then you ran away again before I could talk to you.'

Bruno took another photo out of his wallet.

'You and Philippe only had eyes for each other back then but this is one of the three of us,' and he handed Anna the photograph.

'Oh I remember when this was taken,' Anna exclaimed. 'You had a questionable taste in fluorescent pink socks and trainers in those days,' she laughed.

'Guilty as charged.' And Bruno stuck an elegantly shod foot out for her inspection. 'The name and the socks went a long time ago. Look, my taste is all grown up sophistication now.'

Anna laughed. 'I can see that.'

'Philippe's taste didn't change over the years. He always had very grown up tastes,'

Bruno said, a serious look on his face. 'He always knew what he wanted. You broke his heart, you know,' he added, looking at her.

'I'm sorry about that,' Anna said softly, 'but mine was also fractured irreparably too at the time.'

'Why didn't you return later that summer like you said you would?'

Anna bit her lip. 'I wrote Philippe a letter explaining but he never replied to it, so I assumed he'd changed his mind.'

'Wrong,' Bruno said. 'He did answer it. I know because I posted it for him. But it was returned marked "unknown at this address", six weeks later.'

'He came to England that year too,' Bruno continued quietly. 'Didn't your parents tell you he visited, pleading with them to tell him where you were? They were apparently less than friendly.'

Anna gazed at him, appalled. 'They never told me.'

She was silent for several seconds before saying, 'I'm afraid I was a big disappointment to them — they disowned me in the end.'

'Philippe would never have disowned you. He never forgot you. Oh, he had relationships down the years — he was only human. But nothing serious. No one ever got as close to him as you. He tried to find you for years. I can't believe you work in the film business and your paths never crossed again,' Bruno said shaking his head in disbelief.

'That was a deliberate ploy on my part,' Anna said softly. 'Philippe worked more and more in the States and I made sure I stayed very firmly this side of the pond, in a part of the industry far removed from his. And,' Anna hesitated before looking at Bruno and saying, 'well let's just say I took a couple of extra precautions to make sure I remained incognito. And out of sight of the man who I thought had rejected me.'

'Did you ever marry? Have a family? Meet another special person?' Bruno asked gently.

Anna shook her head. 'No. I've never married. But I've recently met a man who makes me happy like Philippe did all those years ago.'

She twirled the wine in her glass before saying reflectively, 'I've spent my whole adult life regretting my teenage love. It's so cruel that the year I decide to come back to Cannes and make my peace with Philippe, it's too late to talk to him.' She swallowed hard, knowing that once again tears were perilously close.

Bruno handed her a napkin as she fought

to control the tears from falling.

'I did love him you know, totally,' she said. 'I would have done anything he asked me to do.'

'I believe you,' Bruno said quietly.

Anna jumped as her mobile phone rang in the silence that followed his words.

'Excuse me,' she said, pressing the answer button.

'Leo, darling. Everything all right?'

'My flight was early. I'm about ten minutes away from the villa — are you there?'

'No. I'm in Cannes having lunch with . . . with an old friend,' Anna said, smiling at Bruno. 'I'll meet you at the villa in about a quarter of an hour.'

Switching her phone off Anna turned to Bruno.

'I'm so sorry but I have to go. Listen, why don't you come to the party I'm giving on Tuesday night? Bring a guest if you like. I'll get Rick to send you an invite, shall I? We can finish our talk then. Thank you for a lovely lunch,' and Anna stood up to go.

'I'm sorry you have to rush off,' Bruno said also standing up. 'We still have a lot of catching up to do. But yes, I would like to come to your party next week.'

'Good,' Anna said. 'I look forward to introducing you to Leo.'

A serious look crossed Bruno's face as he studied her before saying, 'Anna before you go, was there something in particular you were hoping to talk to Philippe about? Or was it just a question of ending a forty year silence?'

Anna hesitated, torn between telling Bruno the truth now and wanting to tell Leo first.

Bruno, sensing her hesitation stretched his hand out to hold and squeeze Anna's hand in a conciliatory gesture.

'Whatever, I feel I must warn you about something that is likely to come to a head in the next few days.'

Anna looked at him and waited for him to continue.

'The Cambone family are investigating a couple of letters that Philippe received in the weeks before he died. Letters relating to the Cambone family tree. Apparently the person who wrote them is here in Cannes for the festival and has asked to meet with Jacques urgently.'

As Anna stared at him, Bruno continued. 'It seems Philippe's integrity and legacy are about to be questioned.'

CHAPTER 8

'Right I'm off,' Daisy said. 'Not sure what time I'll be back, so don't wait up.'

'Not wearing jeans tonight then?' Poppy said. 'You look nice in that dress, by the way.'

Daisy looked down at herself self-consciously and shrugged. 'Fancied a change. Oh, Leo's coming over,' Daisy said, looking past her sister towards the villa garden.

Poppy turned. 'Oh dear, I hope nothing is wrong,' she added anxiously, moving towards the kitchen door to greet Leo.

'Sorry to disturb you, Poppy, Daisy,' Leo said. 'But I was wondering if you had an ice bucket? I've bought some champagne for this evening and need something to keep it cool on the table.'

'Sure,' Poppy answered, taking a silver ice bucket from one of the cupboards and handing it to Leo.

'Would you like some extra ice as well?'

Leo shook his head. 'No. Thanks for this,' and he turned to go back to the villa.

'Wonder if he's planning to celebrate something in particular,' Daisy said.

'Probably just celebrating being together down here,' Poppy answered. 'You'll be late for the stars arriving at the screening if you don't get going. Enjoy the film with Nat.'

As usual Cannes port was busy and Daisy had to dodge the crowds as she made her way to the front of the Palais des Festivals to watch the stars arriving for the evening screening.

A friendly policeman let her squeeze through the barrier when she showed him her press pass and she stood on her tiptoes in the middle of the Croisette, trying to see over the crowds and record her impressions.

The usual herd of paparazzi were busy snapping away, strident voices urging the stars to, 'Look this way. Turn your head, love. Stand still,' while the precious jewels they wore dazzled under the barrage of flashlights that sought to capture every detail.

The film showing that evening was a popular 'boy's own adventure' and the appearance of the ruggedly handsome male star was greeted with delight by the crowd.

Mentally Daisy made a note of his co-star's glamorous evening gown — an off-the-shoulder white affair with a sequinned bodice that clung to her body — and the stunning ruby necklace she was wearing.

As the stars made their way slowly up the red carpet towards the entrance, Daisy scrutinized the paparazzi for a glimpse of Marcus but couldn't see him.

A limousine, the French flag flying on the bonnet, drew up at the foot of the steps, discharging a government minister and his wife in whom nobody was really interested; their progress up the steps, flanked by security men, was quick and over in minutes.

Guessing that all the 'A list' celebrities were now in the Palais waiting for the screening to begin, Daisy began to make her way towards the beach cinema and Nat.

A happy party atmosphere pervaded the length of the Croisette as the lights began to shine in the twilight; entertainers were still juggling and singing to the crowds.

Nat was waiting for her by the entrance to the beach cinema, a small black rucksack on his back.

'Hi. Sorry if I'm late,' Daisy said. 'I had to do some star watching for my next report.'

'No problem,' Nat said, kissing her on the

cheek. A kiss that was somehow totally different from the ones that Marcus had been insisting on giving her. 'Let's find somewhere to sit,' and taking her by the hand, he lead the way down on to the beach.

As they settled themselves down, Daisy glanced at Nat. 'You OK? You seem a bit quiet tonight.'

'Sorry,' Nat apologized. 'I'm fine. It's just,' he hesitated. 'Have you seen Marcus today?'

'No. Why? Is something wrong with him? He wasn't outside the Palais earlier.'

'No, I don't think there's anything wrong,' Nat hastened to reassure her. 'It's just that . . .'

Nat looked at Daisy seriously before asking, 'Are you two an item away from work?' He paused before continuing, 'I really like you Daisy and want to get to know you better but I don't want to butt in if you're in a relationship. I'm kind of old fashioned like that.'

Daisy smiled and shook her head as Nat looked at her anxiously. So he had got the wrong idea from all those French style cheek kisses he'd witnessed Marcus giving her.

'Nat — Marcus and I are work colleagues, that's all. We've never been out on a proper date together.'

'You sure?'

Daisy nodded. 'Yes.'

'Only, I saw Marcus earlier, by the way. Getting up close and personal with one of the stylists working for Dior. They're having dinner together tonight at the Palm Beach.'

Daisy shrugged. 'Nat, I really couldn't care less what Marcus gets up to — or who he sleeps with.' Should she tell Nat about Ben and Australia? Not tonight, she decided. It was too soon. When she knew him better. Besides Ben was too far away to worry about.

Nat took her hand. 'Good. You're looking very pretty tonight by the way.'

'Thank you,' Daisy said smiling. 'Any news on your script?'

Nat shook his head. 'Not yet. Teddy Wickham has been too busy to do anything yet but keeps promising he will when he gets "a window in his schedule" sometime next week.' Nat shrugged resignedly. 'In the meantime, I'm trying to make a few contacts of my own.'

'Hey, want to come to Anna's party next week? I'm sure I can get you an invite and she's on the production side of things so who knows who might be there. It's Tuesday night. Can you get the evening off?'

'Not a problem. I can always bribe Jasmine the housekeeper with a box of chocolates to babysit that evening,' Nat said. 'You sure Anna won't mind?'

'Pretty certain,' Daisy said. 'I'll ask her tomorrow and let you know. Can I ask you a personal question?'

'Yes.'

'How did you become a nanny? I know these days anyone can do anything they want but you must admit it's still pretty unusual to find male nannies.'

'Well firstly, I'm not a nanny. I'm a Montessori trained nursery teacher. I knew I'd have to do something to earn a living while I tried to sell my scripts and I love kids — particularly three to seven year olds, they're fun to be around. And before you ask, the job with the Wickhams for the festival came about via a friend of a friend. Normally I freelance through an agency. Leaves me time to write in between jobs.

'Right, now we've cleared that up, I've got a bottle of champagne in here,' Nat said opening the rucksack and taking a bottle and two glasses out.

'Do you know what the classic film is tonight?' she asked, holding the glasses while Nat skilfully opened the champagne.

'Well, it's not Tom and Jerry, that's for sure. It's *Dirty Harry* — if you don't like gangster films we don't have to stay.' Nat glanced at her.

'We can always leave and find a quiet spot to drink this and just watch the sea.'

'What, and miss Clint Eastwood uttering those immortal words: "Make my day"?' Daisy laughed. 'He's here at the festival this year, isn't he?'

Nat nodded. 'Yes he's got a film showing and he's . . .' Nat's voice trailed away as he looked beyond Daisy. 'He's actually walking towards the screen. He's going to make a speech about the film by the look of things.'

They both listened as Clint talked about his 1971 film. His remark, 'If you have trouble recognizing me, I'm the one with the brown hair and lots of it,' said with a self-deprecating smile, delighted the crowd and earned him a round of applause as the film began and he left.

Sitting on the beach next to Nat, Daisy found it hard to concentrate on the film. If she were honest *Dirty Harry* wasn't really her kind of film — she was more a *Sleepless in Seattle* type of girl. Sitting companionably at Nat's side, she let not only the rolling sound of the Mediterranean as it lapped at the beach, wash over her, but also much of the film's dialogue and action as she thought about the future and Ben's letter.

Thinking he'd made a mistake wasn't the same as knowing and regretting, was it? He hadn't actually mentioned loving her in the letter, just that he was missing her. And did he seriously expect her to go halfway around the world on a whim of his? Probably, she decided. Ben had always been the one to decide what they would do as a couple and she'd tended to follow meekly in his wake.

She'd quite enjoyed her independence of the last few months — particularly once she'd got over the shock of Ben dumping her and re-discovered some of her own dreams. So much had been pushed to one side while she was with Ben.

Like going freelance. 'No security in being a freelance,' Ben had said. 'We both need a regular monthly cheque.'

Now she was alone, was she brave enough to go freelance? Unlike Nat she didn't have any other training to fall back on. She did have some savings though. Enough to live on for at least six months, she reckoned, if the freelance work didn't take off straight away.

When the cooling night air made her shiver and Nat placed an arm protectively around her shoulders, she snuggled in against him. Right now she realized, she was happier than she'd been in years. She didn't need Ben in her life.

As the credits rolled Nat asked, 'Taxi or shall we walk back?'

'Let's walk along the bord de mer,' Daisy answered. 'It's such a lovely evening.'

Late though it was, the restaurants along the bord de mer were still busy — there were even a few brave souls going for a late night dip. Strolling along with her arm around Nat's waist and his arm around her shoulders felt comfortable and natural. As did the goodnight kiss he gave her as he left her at the villa door. A delicious tingling feeling flooded through her body.

'Goodnight, Daisy. See you tomorrow. Thank you for a lovely evening.'

As Daisy watched him go with a smile on her face, she realized with that kiss, Nat had just 'made her day'.

Anna, putting the finishing touches to the special dinner she'd prepared, glanced out of the kitchen window to where Leo was busy organizing things around the pool. He didn't seem disappointed that they were eating at the villa tonight instead of finding a special restaurant as he'd initially suggested.

'A romantic dinner with just the two of us here, will be wonderful,' he'd said. 'So long as it's not too much trouble for you.'

'I love having someone special to cook for,' Anna had answered.

Watching Leo light the candles on the table and adjust the chairs, Anna felt a wave of love wash over her. She was so lucky to have met Leo. Picking up their smoked salmon starters she took them outside and placed them on the table.

Standing there with the candles and the sonar garden lights flickering into life and the occasional bat flitting through the twilight, Anna looked at Leo, and said softly, 'I need to talk to you.'

Moving to her side, Leo took her in his arms. 'In a minute. First, I love you — will you marry me?'

Although she'd been longing to hear that very question for some months, she hadn't expected Leo to choose this particular evening to voice it and Anna looked at him in wonder before whispering, 'Yes. If you'll have me after we've talked.'

'Shh, there is nothing you can tell me that will stop me loving you,' Leo said seriously. 'Now, where's the ring?' and he took a small box out of his pocket. The ruby and diamond ring he slipped on her finger was a perfect fit and Anna touched it in wonder.

'It's beautiful, thank you.'

'Beautiful like you, my darling,' Leo said

119

before kissing her.

Later as they sat sipping the champagne he had fetched from the kitchen, Leo asked, 'So, what's the verdict on your return to Cannes? Has it been a success for you so far? Laid the ghost that has haunted your life so far?'

Anna shook her head. 'No not really. Shall we just say the current situation is fluid.' She looked at Leo. 'I want you to meet Bruno.'

'This is the old friend you had lunch with?'

Anna nodded. 'I think you'll like him. He's Philippe's best friend from years ago and they are, were, still close. He was called Brian in those days. He told me things I didn't know. Philippe thought I'd rejected him, when I was convinced he'd rejected me. Bruno told me how Philippe had tried to find me.'

Anna was quiet for several seconds before adding quietly, 'My late parents don't come out of this well, but,' she shrugged. 'I can't challenge them about it now. I suppose they did what they believed to be right at the time.'

Thoughtfully she twirled the champagne in her glass and watched the bubbles plop on the surface before taking a deep breath and saying, 'I had Philippe Cambone's baby. And I had to give him away.'

Leo leant forward and gently wiped away the tears that were starting to fall down Anna's cheeks.

'Oh my darling, that must have been so hard for you.'

Anna nodded, unable to speak as she tried to stem the tears.

'I'd sort of guessed there was more to your relationship with Philippe than you'd told me,' Leo said. 'But you having a baby all alone and having to give it up, didn't cross my mind.'

'I wrote to him when I found out I was pregnant but I didn't hear from him so I assumed he'd changed his mind about me. That he didn't love me like he said. I waited and waited, hoping to hear from him, but the moment my parents realized "my condition", all hell broke loose.'

'The swinging sixties didn't embrace everyone did they?' Leo said.

'Certainly not my parents. I was bundled off to a home for wayward girls and told if I kept the baby I was to never darken their doors again,' Anna said. 'Seems unbelievable now in this day and age doesn't it?' She shook her head.

'Anyway, when Jean-Philippe — that's what I called my son — was twenty-four hours old I had to say goodbye and hand him over for adoption.' Anna bit her lip at the memory of that moment. 'I've had no contact with him from that day to this. I had hoped when the adoption privacy laws changed a few years ago, he would get in touch but,' she shrugged her shoulders despondently. 'I guess he's happy without me, the mother who gave him away, in his life.'

'I can't believe you've worked in the film industry for so long and not bumped into Philippe Cambone,' Leo said. 'That all this hasn't come out before.'

Anna shrugged. 'Bruno said the same. But it's such a vast industry and I made sure I was in a totally different section of it. Besides, a lot of Philippe's work was in the States and I stayed this side of the Atlantic.'

She glanced at Leo. 'I did follow his career for years. In the beginning I couldn't help myself. I had to know what he was doing. I even went to a lecture he gave one year at the Film Institute in London, just to be close to him. It was torture and I never did it again.'

Anna was silent for a moment, taking the handkerchief Leo had used to gently wipe her cheeks and twisting it into knots.

'Yesterday Bruno mentioned something.

Apparently just before he died Philippe received a letter from someone suggesting they were related, and asking to meet him during the festival. Philippe had agreed to a meeting but no firm date was arranged. The Cambones are worried now there may be an unexpected claim against Philippe's estate.'

Anna bit her lip as she looked at Leo.

'Do you think this person could be my son?'

'Oh Anna, my darling, anything is possible but don't get your hopes up too high. Did Bruno give you a name or anything? Indicate what the relationship was? Who'd written the letter?'

'No. You rang and I left before I could ask him any questions,' Anna said.

'To think I'd almost come to terms with the fact that I would never see my son again,' Anna said. 'But now, suddenly, I've got hope.'

Leo sighed as he gently stroked her hand. 'Don't raise your hopes too high, my darling,' he said quietly. 'Yes, it could be Philippe's child seeking to establish his roots but it doesn't necessarily mean that it will be your child. Philippe could have had a relationship with somebody else during the last forty years.'

'I know, I know,' Anna said, before whispering, 'But wouldn't it be wonderful if it was my Jean-Philippe?'

CHAPTER 9

After a restless night Anna woke the next morning to the sound of rain splattering against the windows.

Quickly she pushed the covers back and swung her legs out of bed. This was the South of France, it shouldn't be raining, especially not today with the premiere of *Future Promises* tonight. The one thing she didn't need was a walk up the red carpet in the rain.

The smell of coffee was wafting upstairs and she could hear Leo in the kitchen whistling happily. Shrugging herself into her housecoat, Anna made her way downstairs.

Leo turned as she entered the kitchen. 'Good morning, my darling. Coffee?'

'Please. I can't believe it's raining,' Anna said.

'Forecast is for it to clear by midday,' Leo said reassuringly. 'Now, what's our timetable for today?' he asked, handing her a mug of coffee.

'Hairdresser for me this morning; there is some jewellery being delivered here this afternoon at about five o'clock then a limo arrives at seven to takes us to town.'

'So, nothing major for me to get involved with?' Leo asked.

Anna shook her head. 'No. Is there something you'd like to do? We could have lunch in town after my hair do is finished if you like. The restaurant I met Bruno in yesterday was very good.'

'OK. I'll book us a table.'

'Talking of Bruno,' Anna hesitated, not sure how Leo would react to her next words. 'I'm going to ring and ask him to tell me the name of this person who has contacted the Cambones — if he knows it.'

'Oh Anna, d'you think that's wise? Why not wait until after the premiere at least. After this evening you'll be able to relax and deal with . . . well, deal with whatever the remaining week of the Festival throws at you.'

'I just want to know the name,' Anna said. 'But you're right. I'll wait until after the premiere. We'll enjoy the party tonight.'

'Does Bruno know about the true depth

of your relationship with Philippe?' Leo asked.

Anna shook her head. 'Not sure. You're the first person I've ever told. Though from the way he was talking yesterday, I think Bruno may have some idea. Philippe obviously talked to him about me.'

They both turned as there was a gentle knock on the door.

Daisy apologized when Anna opened the door.

'Anna, I'm sorry to bother you so early but I need to ask you a couple of favours.'

Anna looked at her warily.

'First, your party on Tuesday. Could my friend Nat possibly come? He's a script-writer trying to make some contacts. At the moment he's had to resort to taking a nanny job — oh I think you met Cindy the other day didn't you? She's Verity Raymond's daughter and Nat's looking after her while her parents are at the festival; her father's on the jury.'

'Of course Nat may come. He should be able to make a few contacts if nothing else. I'll try and introduce him to as many people as I can,' Anna said generously. 'The other favour?'

'My editor e-mailed me this morning. He's heard a rumour that Johnny Depp is to star as Tonto in a remake of *The Lone Ranger* and says that if Johnny is in town I'm to get an interview with him. As if!' Daisy shook her head. 'But he's definitely putting the pressure on for me to come up with something, so I was wondering if you'd thought any more about walking around Cannes with me and giving me the before and after picture?' Daisy looked hopefully at Anna. 'Tomorrow morning would be good for me.'

'Oh Daisy, I really don't know,' Anna said sighing.

'Any reason why I shouldn't tag along?' Leo asked unexpectedly. 'I'd be interested in hearing your reminiscences first hand. Would you mind?' he asked turning to Daisy.

'No I don't mind,' Daisy answered. 'Especially if it would make Anna feel better about doing it?' and she looked at Anna questioningly.

'OK,' Anna smiled. 'I give in. Although I'm still not sure that I'm going to remember anything of importance — or even of interest. It was all so long ago.'

'Great. Thanks Anna. Eleven o'clock outside the Palais des Festival tomorrow morning all right for you then? Enjoy the premiere tonight. Really hope the rain clears up for you.'

The weather forecast was right. The rain did stop and by the evening as Anna and Leo prepared for their appearance on the red carpet, it was dry, even if the breeze was on the chilly side.

Anna handed the diamond and sapphire necklace that had been delivered to the villa earlier that afternoon to Leo. 'Could you do the catch, please? I'm terrified I won't do it up properly and I'll lose it. I dread to think how much it's worth.'

'It's rather lovely isn't it?' Leo said as he carefully did up the clasp and double checked it. 'The sapphires match your dress perfectly.'

'Does my dress look all right?' Anna asked anxiously. 'I wasn't sure when I bought it whether it was too fitted for me. And these sandals,' she glanced down at the silver strappy shoes with their five-inch heels. 'They're not too high are they?'

'Anna, Anna,' Leo said as he turned her round to face him and gently kissed her.

'You look beautiful tonight, my darling. Your dress, your hair, your shoes — everything is perfect. Now, relax and try to enjoy the evening.'

Standing in the circle of his arms, Anna

smiled. 'I'll try. Having you here makes it very special. Have I told you how handsome you're looking tonight?'

Leo shook his head. 'We make such a perfect couple!' he said laughing and delicately traced the outline of her face with his fingers before gently kissing her again.

As a brisk toot of a car horn sounded outside, Leo placed Anna's white fake fur shrug around her shoulders, before picking up and handing her the small beaded clutch handbag she'd decided to use and taking her by the arm.

'The red carpet awaits — let's go.'

Sitting next to Leo as the limousine made its way towards the Palais des Festivals, Anna checked the contents of her bag: lipstick, comb, tissue and her locket. It was the first time for years that the gold locket wasn't around her neck but the diamond and sapphire necklace had to take precedence tonight.

'Relax and enjoy the evening,' Leo whispered as the limousine came to a halt at the foot of the famous steps. A burly security man opened the car door and together Anna and Leo stepped onto the red carpet.

Nothing had prepared Anna for the noise and the exuberance of the large crowds lining the Croisette and along the front of the

Palais. Four or five deep in places behind the barriers, she could see people standing on stools, several strategically placed ladders, all hoping for a better view of the stars as they arrived. Leo took her hand as several flashlights went off.

'Who do they think we are?' Anna whispered to Leo.

'Someone very famous obviously — you're looking so glamorous tonight,' Leo said, pulling her towards him and kissing her to the delight of the crowd.

Rick was waiting for them on the red carpet, standing slightly to one side of the stairs. 'Anna, you look stunning. Nice to see you, Leo. Helen and Rupert should be here in a moment,' he said. 'Then it will be our turn to walk the walk and face the paparazzi.'

'The atmosphere is amazing,' Anna said, looking around. To her left a couple of television reporters were facing cameramen and talking rapidly into microphones detailing the scene before them, announcing the names of the famous stars as they arrived and describing the sumptuous gowns and jewellery.

Further up the steps Anna caught a glimpse of Bruno being approached by another reporter with a cameraman in tow.

She'd forgotten Bruno was a big name down here and his thoughts on the festival would obviously be sought after by the media.

The gentle pressure of Leo's hand in hers, brought her attention back to their own group and she smiled apologetically at Leo.

'Sorry,' she whispered. 'That's Bruno up there.'

Leo followed her gaze. 'Oh.'

'I wonder what he's talking about to the TV reporter,' Anna said. 'Ah, here's Rupert and Helen,' she added, as a silver limousine drew up.

Watching the two young stars of *Future Promises* arrive on the red carpet, Anna felt a surge of affection for both of them. A couple of people in the crowd realizing who they were, called out their names, 'Rupert, Helen love, can we have your autographs?' Smiling happily the two went over and graciously signed the offered magazines, books and cards.

Finally they all linked arms and began to make their way up the paparazzi lined flight of steps through a barrage of flashlight. As they drew level with Bruno on the last of the red carpeted stairs and went to enter the Palais itself, Anna couldn't help overhearing the interviewer say, 'Finally Bruno, can you shed any light on this latest development in the Philippe Cambone saga? I know you two were very close. Were you aware of this secret family he had in the States?'

Anna gasped involuntarily as she heard the question and would have fallen if Leo's grip on her arm hadn't tightened and saved her as she stumbled, trying unsuccessfully to hear Bruno's reply. Leo looked at her concerned.

'Anna, are you okay? They're waiting to show us to our seats.'

'I'm fine,' Anna said, gripping Leo's hand tightly. 'Lead on.'

It was gone nine o'clock when Anna woke the next morning. She lay there for a few moments re-living the exciting events of the previous night. So many people, so many congratulations, so much champagne.

The general consensus was that *Future Promises* was about to be a big hit at the box office and earn world wide recognition for its young stars. Consequently Helen and Rupert had been the toast of Cannes last night. Anna, delighted for them, had enjoyed basking in the reflected glory.

The theme of the after-screening party — 'Future Promises — What's Yours?' — had proved to be a major hit. The venue, draped and decorated like a mystical sheikh's tent, with zodiac signs, huge silver moons and stars hanging from the pleated ceiling and large golden suns shining from the walls, had been a perfect setting for a fun evening of make believe and fortune telling.

There was a wheel of fortune, origami fortune tellers, fortune sticks, Chinese fortune cookies, astrology readings and even a Romany gypsy complete with bunches of lavender and a crystal ball in a curtained booth for those that fancied a personal consultation.

Partygoers eagerly entered into the spirit of things as a king's fool and jester cavorted around making mischief and encouraging everyone to join in the fun. Music had been provided disco-style by a young DJ and the whole evening had been as Leo said later in the limousine going home, 'A night to remember for all the right reasons.'

Anna had seen the gypsy fortune teller in her booth early in the evening and had been tempted to have her gaze into the crystal ball on her behalf then, but the number of people already waiting had put her off. It was two o'clock in the morning as she and Leo swayed to a last smoochy dance tune when she saw 'Cassandra' sitting alone in her booth.

'I know it's silly,' she said glancing at Leo. 'But shall we? Just for fun.'

Smiling Leo led her by the hand over to the gypsy woman's booth. 'You go in and see what she has to say. I'm going to organize our car home.'

Cassandra looked up as Anna hesitated at the entrance to the booth, suddenly not sure that she wanted to do this.

'I'm sorry — am I too late?'

Cassandra smiled, shaking her head as she beckoned her in. 'Please, sit.'

Anna sat down in front of the round table with its scarlet velvet covering and watched apprehensively as Cassandra gazed trance-like at her crystal ball before starting to speak.

'Although something from the past is making waves in your life at the moment, you are entering a very happy period. I see a man who loves you and wants to take care of you in the future. Through him the family life you've always dreamed of will be yours, I see grandchildren — a little girl holding a toddler by the hand — families coming together. A journey of some sort. The past embracing the future.'

Cassandra paused and looked up at Anna before adding quietly, 'Do not mourn the past, nor worry about the future, live the present moment wisely and earnestly.'

Now, re-living the scene with Cassandra in her mind on Monday morning, Anna knew the gypsy had told her nothing that she didn't already know. She knew she loved Leo as much as he loved her and knew they would be happy together, that his family would become hers, his grandchildren, hers. But as for the past embracing the future — what did that mean?

As the picture of Cassandra in her booth faded from her mind, Anna slipped out of bed and, pulling on her housecoat, tiptoed out of the room and went downstairs.

Her mobile phone was on the kitchen work surface and she picked it up before unlocking the door and stepping out on to the terrace. Sitting in one of the cane chairs Poppy had placed out there, Anna opened her phone and scrolled down until she found the number she wanted and pressed the dial button. As the connection was being processed, Anna tensed, her whole body rigid with expectation, her fingers playing with the locket chain that was once again around her neck.

'Bonjour. Who is this?'

'It's Anna,' she said quickly. 'I need to talk to you.'

'I'm listening.'

'You didn't tell me Philippe had a secret family in the States.'

'That's because he didn't,' Bruno said.

'But that reporter last night, at the Palais?'

Anna could hear Bruno's deep sigh down the telephone. 'The press, as usual, have got hold of the wrong end of the stick, Anna. They've heard about the possibility of a claim against the estate and have jumped to conclusions. Philippe did NOT have a family he kept secret from everyone. I told you not having a family was the biggest regret of his life. He would have adored having children.'

'Bruno?' Anna hesitated.

'Will you tell me the name of the person who wrote to Philippe please?'

There was a pause before Bruno answered.

'Oh Anna. I'm not sure that I should before the Cambones make the name public.'

'Okay. If I put it another way, maybe you can answer me.' Anna took a deep breath before continuing.

'Does the signature on the letters contain the name Jean-Philippe? Or is it mentioned in the letter anywhere? Yes or no?'

'I'm sorry Anna, that name is not a part of the signature on the letters, Jacques showed me. Neither is it in the letter itself,' Bruno said gently. 'I can tell you the letters were from a woman,' he added quietly. 'Not a man.'

Anna, unable to bear the message concealed behind his words, twisted her fingers round and round in her locket chain until it was cutting into her. As, sad and frustrated, she pulled at the chain trying to untangle it, the chain broke and the locket fell to the floor.

'Thank you Bruno,' Anna managed to whisper as she pressed the off button on the phone before beginning to sob uncontrollably as she picked up her broken locket.

She was still crying when Leo found her ten minutes later, her face red and blotched, the locket and its broken chain clutched in her hand.

'I'm sorry,' she sobbed as Leo took her in his arms to comfort her. 'I'd pinned my hopes on it being Jean-Philippe who had contacted Philippe. But Bruno has just told me it's a woman. Which means it's not my son who wrote to him.'

CHAPTER 10

'Good morning, Poppy,' Daisy said, running downstairs into the kitchen early Monday morning. 'You look busy already.'

Poppy groaned as she looked up from a list she was writing. 'You'll definitely be around to help me tomorrow won't you? This party is getting out of hand.'

'I promised didn't I?' Daisy said, helping herself to a banana from the fruit bowl on the table. 'What's the problem anyway?'

'Everything! I'm spending the day cooking the savoury stuff — I'll do the desserts tomorrow. And there's still so much to organize. Leo and Anna are now planning to officially announce their engagement at the party, so would I please organize a cake and more champagne. At a day's notice. Oh, and they want an official photographer.'

'Poppy, calm down. This is France remember. Every patisserie on every street corner has wonderful cakes, not to mention the supermarchés. We'll get one of those and I'll ice it into an engagement cake. OK? And the photographer is not a problem either. Marcus has already asked if he can come, so now he can — officially.' Daisy threw the banana skin into the compost bin under the sink.

'Tell me more about the engagement. That must have been what the champagne was for the other evening. Have you seen Anna's ring?'

Poppy shook her head. 'No. And the quick glimpse I did get of Anna earlier, I thought she looked rather subdued.'

'Too much partying after the premiere I expect,' Daisy said cheerfully.

'Expect so,' Poppy answered, absently writing something on a list. 'I'll order an extra fifty champagne glasses for the engagement toast and sixty wine glasses in total. D'you think that's enough? People do hang on to their glass don't they, rather than taking a fresh one each time?'

Poppy took a deep breath and ticked something on her list. 'The pianist is coming this afternoon to check the piano over. I just hope the weather is OK tomorrow evening. I've got extra candles to put around the place, and some floating ones for the pool. Oh! Nobody is going to want to swim are they?' She looked up at Daisy anxiously.

'Not when they're all dressed up in their glad rags. Look, I've got to go into Cannes now. I have to see Marcus and then I'm meeting up with Anna and Leo at eleven o'clock. Anna's finally agreed to help me with my 'Then and Now' feature,' she explained sensing Poppy's unspoken question. 'But I'll definitely be back mid-afternoon and we'll make a start on getting everything sorted. OK?'

Walking into Cannes, Daisy thought about the feature she planned to write with the help of Anna's memories about the twenty-first Festival. She'd already found a few archive photos of Cannes back in the 1960s to go alongside some of Marcus's modern day shots. Hopefully Anna would have some nostalgic anecdotes about her first visit to the Festival. If not, Daisy decided, she'd make it more of a photo feature with just a few words comparing the old and new pictures.

Before starting to look for Marcus in the Village International on the quay, Daisy found an empty seat in the gardens near the Hotel de Ville and switched on her recorder.

'The rain clouds have gone and once again the sky is a clear azure blue. It's hard to believe that already the Festival is entering its second week. The days have simply flown by. But people are still partying and networking in the cafés and bars and along the Croisette people are desperately strutting their stuff knowing that time is running out. The presenting of the Palm d'Or is only days away but still the hype continues. Will it be like the year when the very last film to be premiered won the coveted award? Or have we already seen the winner?' Daisy spoke quietly into her tape recorder as she watched a fire-eater entertain a small crowd.

'Today is the private funeral of Philippe Cambone, the famous film producer, born in Cannes, who died suddenly last week. Flags are expected to fly at half-mast this morning but industry VIPs will have to wait to pay their respects at a memorial service to be held after the Festival ends.' Thoughtfully Daisy switched off her recorder.

She'd get another report e-mailed to the paper today, write up her 'Then and Now' feature tonight and then tomorrow she'd help Poppy all day and enjoy the party in the evening. Now to find Marcus. She needed to make sure he still wanted to come to Anna's party tomorrow and that he was available — didn't have a hot date with a blonde.

'Great. I'll definitely be there,' he said,

when Daisy tracked him down in the American marquee in the Village International.

'Enjoy your dinner at the Palm Beach the other night?' Daisy enquired casually.

'Yes thank you. You and Nat have a good evening?' Marcus returned equally casually.

Daisy nodded. 'Thanks. Marcus, I think we're going to have to forget that dinner on Bill's expenses.'

Marcus looked at her, his eyes narrowed. 'Why?'

Daisy shrugged. 'I seem to be running out of time. Things are so hectic down here. Like you said, there's always so much going on. Besides, I think it's better if we just keep things on a working basis. So no more of those kissy kissy French greetings either. OK?'

'Nothing to do with Nat, this?' Marcus asked.

'Nothing. Nat and I are just friends,' Daisy said. 'Good friends but nothing more.' She had no intention of placing Nat in a difficult position with Marcus while they were down here — after all it had been Marcus who introduced them. What happened after the Festival finished was another matter altogether.

'I've heard from Ben,' she said quietly. 'He wants me to join him in Sydney.'

Working in the same office Marcus would have heard all about how Ben had left her. If he wanted to believe there was more behind her words than was the case, that was up to him. It would at least put a stop to any ideas he might have had about the two of them getting together while they were down here.

Lazily floating on her back in the villa swimming pool before preparing to go indoors to shower and meet Daisy in town, Anna tried to marshal her thoughts.

Tired after the premiere and the party and emotionally drained after her conversation with Bruno, she desperately wanted to be able to concentrate on the present, on Leo, on their future together.

Leo was keen to make plans — engagement announcement, wedding, honeymoon, christening, Christmas. Family plans. Plans for the future that suddenly Anna couldn't face making. She'd successfully buried the past deep inside her for so many years, refusing to acknowledge what had happened, and wishing she could find love again. So now with Leo in her life, why couldn't she simply embrace their love and move forward?

Anna sighed inwardly, knowing the answer. By coming to Cannes this year she'd demolished the fragile emotional dam wall she'd built around herself over the years and unleashed a veritable flood-tide of evocative thoughts and feelings.

If only Philippe hadn't died and she'd been able to make her peace with him face to face she would have been able to make plans for her future with Leo with more composure. Wouldn't she?

Anna turned on to her front and began to swim slowly towards the pool-side steps. All these ifs. If she wasn't careful her past would drive a wedge between her and Leo.

Once out of the water she slipped into her towelling robe, resolutely tying the belt around her waist. The past was over and done with; the sooner she accepted that Philippe was dead and that Jean-Philippe would never be a part of her life however much she wished for it, the better. She'd treat today's walk around Cannes as a cathartic exercise — dig as deep as she could into her memories, expose them to scrutiny and finally exorcise them. Then she'd get on with the rest of her life with Leo.

The Croisette was crowded with sightseers when Anna and Leo arrived and it took them several moments to find Daisy who was still talking to Marcus near the foot of the Palais steps.

'Hi. This is Marcus — he's agreed to be your official photographer on Tuesday,' Daisy said introducing them.

'Official photographer?' Anna said surprised. 'I don't think we need one.'

'I asked Poppy to find us one,' Leo explained. 'I'd like some engagement pictures to show the family when we get back. And I'm sure Rick and the rest of the office would like some memento of the party.'

'See you Tuesday then,' Marcus said. 'Just had a tip-off that Madonna is coming ashore at the Palm Beach so I need to get down there asap.'

As Marcus left, Daisy turned to Anna and Leo. 'Congratulations to you two by the way. May I see the ring? Oh that's so beautiful,' she said, as Anna held out her hand. 'Have you set a date for the wedding?'

'Not yet,' Leo answered. 'I'm trying to persuade Anna sooner rather than later. A summer wedding would be nice.'

Anna laughed. 'Leo doesn't realize just how much organizing even a quiet wedding takes,' she explained to Daisy. 'I think September is probably the earliest, but we shall see. Now, where shall we start this trip down memory lane?'

'Other side of the road outside the hotel that stands on the old Palais site and make our way along inwards to the centre of town?' Daisy suggested.

As they dodged past cars, scooters and an open-top bus to cross the road, Anna said, 'There was less traffic around in those days, that's for sure. The crowds are different too.'

'How?'

'Older and more middle-class. In '68 there were lots of students — of which I was one. It was not nearly so colourful then either,' Anna said looking at a particularly garish gold and silver window display. 'I found it all rather intimidating, particularly as the news of the Paris riots filtered down and there were demonstrations. Philippe wanted to get involved — did get involved — but I was too scared, particularly after I nearly got trampled.'

'Philippe? Trampled?' Daisy asked.

'My job at the festival was to act as general dogsbody and messenger between the various companies and film studios who were down here,' Anna explained. 'One morning when I was trying to deliver some film tapes I got caught up in a student protest. Actually, it was just along here, past the Carlton. I slipped off the pavement, twisted my ankle and fell over as the students broke through the barriers the police had erected and surged forward towards the palais. Philippe left the crowd when he saw me sitting on the pavement nursing my leg and helped me move to safety. Refused to leave me.' Anna smiled.

'Was this Philippe Cambone?' Daisy asked slowly.

'Yes,' Anna said. 'I'm sorry, Daisy. I didn't lie to you when you asked if I'd ever worked with him — I hadn't. But I should have told you I did know him back then.

'Meeting Philippe changed my life. For six days he showed me another world. Growing up in a quiet Devonshire village I'd never experienced a place like Cannes. Never realized how different other people's lives could be,' Anna said, glancing around.

'Philippe was very French in his support of the students and took me to several meetings wanting me to get involved.'

She shrugged. 'How could I? I didn't speak the language for a start, and secondly I was going home at the end of the Festival. Back to art college and a different life.'

A couple of council workers were preparing to erect some temporary barriers across the road and gesticulated to them to walk through quickly.

'Despite the unrest and the protests it was

a lot easier to get close to people in those days. Security was very low key, virtually non-existent. I saw, and in some cases even met, people like Ringo Starr and George Harrison. Philippe introduced me to several up and coming stars too. Bridget Bardot was here that year and Orson Welles.' Anna paused as a group of Japanese tourists threatened to run them down in their eagerness to pass along the street before the barriers were in place.

'But when somebody high up in Paris tried to sack the popular Henri Langois, head of Cinématèque Française, the Festival itself erupted into disarray. Suddenly everyone was protesting and boycotting things, jury members were resigning, and there were calls for the festival to close — which of course it did.'

'I found an archive photo of Geraldine Chaplin pulling the curtain across at a screening,' Daisy said. 'Was that the end of the Festival that year?'

Anna nodded. 'End of the Festival yes but the national strikes made it impossible for people to get away. I couldn't leave for another four days.'

'What did you do?'

'Spent most of the time with Philippe. We talked for hours, planning our lives for the next few years.' Anna was quiet for a moment, remembering the intensity of those days. 'The words "Life without Limits" was the phrase on everyone's lips that year. Philippe and I promised ourselves that would be the way we'd live our lives together.' Anna sighed sadly.

'It didn't happen. Philippe was already under contract to work in America for a year. I went back to England and lived another life. A life that has been good to me on the whole and one that has now given me Leo,' Anna said, catching hold of Leo's hand and squeezing it.

'And the future is looking good,' Leo said, drawing her towards him and oblivious of the crowds, kissing her gently.

'Shall we try and make our way to rue d'Antibes? They seem to have closed this road completely for some reason. Can't think why. It's not really anything to do with the Festival,' Daisy said, trying not to envy them their closeness.

'Think maybe that's your answer,' Leo said quietly, moving apart from Anna and watching as a large black limousine drew up behind the barrier in front of the ornate entrance to a church. He tightened his hold of Anna's hand as he felt her tremble.

'Philippe's funeral cortège,' Anna whispered. 'I'd forgotten it was taking place this morning.'

'We'll go this way,' Leo said decisively, leading them into a small alleyway. 'Hopefully we'll come out by the station and we can carry on with our tour.'

CHAPTER 11

'Look what I've got for us,' Daisy said, emptying a carrier bag on to the kitchen table in front of Poppy.

'I had a quick mooch around the shops after I left Anna and Leo this morning. See what I found for us to wear tomorrow evening.'

'So what d'you think?' she said, slipping a velvet and pearl headband around her head. 'Very 1920s don't you think? I thought you'd look great in this hanky-hem dress,' she said, shaking it out and handing it to Poppy.

'I offered to buy Anna and Leo lunch but they said they had some shopping to do and then planned a sandwich lunch,' Daisy said, glancing out across the garden towards the villa. 'Are they back yet?'

'About half an hour ago. Anna went straight indoors and Leo is down by the pool sunbathing,' Poppy answered, holding the dress against herself. 'This is so pretty, thank you. Did Anna remember anything useful?'

Daisy nodded. 'Enough, but it came to an end shortly after we saw the funeral cortège for Philippe Cambone. Anna couldn't seem to concentrate after that.'

Daisy slipped a black beaded jacket over her shoulders. 'I love this.' She glanced at Poppy. 'You remember Anna saying she couldn't help me with reminiscences about Philippe Cambone? Well, this morning she admitted she did know him. In fact, judging from her reaction when we saw the funeral cars, I think there was more to their relationship than she's saying publicly. You should have seen how white she went. Leo was so protective.'

'I have to go across later to finalize some of the arrangements for tomorrow,' Poppy said. 'Hope she's all right. I like Anna.'

'Daisy,' Poppy hesitated. 'I'm afraid when Nat came to collect Tom to play with Cindy, Ben came into the conversation.'

'How?' Daisy took the jacket off and looked at her sister.

'Oh Nat said something about you being a journalist and I flippantly said yes, if she doesn't jack it in to go to Australia. Which seemed to throw him. I take it you haven't mentioned Ben's existence to him?'

'No. It never seemed to be the right moment somehow. Oh by the way I've got an ex boyfriend in Sydney who unexpectedly wants me to join him, isn't easy to drop into the conversation.'

'Doesn't sound that difficult to me if you like someone. Telling them the truth from the beginning is the best policy,' Poppy said.

'Yes, well. It's not a big deal. I'll straighten things out when we take the kids out on Saturday. Promise.'

Daisy folded the jacket and put it in the bag. It was one thing giving Marcus the wrong idea but Nat was different, she really liked him. 'I'll take this lot upstairs and then I'm going to do some work on my laptop, after that I'll be free to help you with things. OK if I work under the loggia? Don't want to be in your way.'

'I'm going to start doing a few table decorations and the flowers before Tom gets back,' Poppy said. 'Could do with a hand when you've finished. The pianist should be here soon to check out the piano. Oh, what about the cake?'

'I've arranged to have one decorated at the supermarché. I'll collect it in the morning,' Daisy said. 'So no worries there.'

Daisy had e-mailed her report and put the

finishing touches to her 'Then and Now' feature before joining Poppy in the kitchen. When Nat returned with Tom and an excited Cindy the two sisters were busy assembling table decorations.

'Tom's coming to my birthday tea and on Saturday Nat's taking us to see the whales, Daisy too,' Cindy told Poppy.

'The Festival will have wound down by then with everyone really just waiting for the winner of the Palm d'Or to be announced,' Nat said. 'So you don't have to worry about missing anything.'

'I'm not worried,' Daisy said. 'You are coming to the party tomorrow night aren't you? I've cleared it with Anna. She's said she'll introduce you to a couple of people.'

'Great. And Teddy Wickham has finally read one of my scripts and wants a producer friend to read it.'

'Nat, that's wonderful,' Daisy said.

'Might mean disappearing to America for a few days or even weeks if they like it,' Nat said. 'Fancy coming with me?' he asked staring at her.

'Aren't you rather rushing things here Nat?' Daisy said.

'I'm sure you'd find plenty to write home about from Los Angeles. Unless you've got other plans? Poppy — and Marcus —

seemed to think you might.'

'Ah. Can we talk about this another time?' Daisy said.

'Tonight? Meet me for a drink later?'

'Oh, I said I'd be at Poppy's beck and call tonight and tomorrow to help with party preparations,' Daisy said. 'I don't know if . . .'

'We're well ahead here,' Poppy said. 'Don't worry on my account.'

'In that case I'll pick you up about eight thirty. Nowhere dressy,' Nat said. 'Come on Cindy. Time we went home.'

Poppy looked at Daisy as the door closed behind them. 'Nat's a good bloke.'

'I know. I really like him. But we've only just met. I can't believe that . . .'

'I knew Dan was the one for me within twenty-four hours of meeting him,' Poppy interrupted. 'Trust your instincts for once.'

Leo and Anna were sitting on the terrace after supper when Leo reached into his pocket and placed a small package on the table. 'Before I forget. I got you something in town earlier,' he said. 'Where's your locket?'

'Upstairs in my purse,' Anna replied, opening the tissue wrapped package to find a gold chain nestling within its folds. 'Oh

156

thank you. I'll get the locket.'

Returning a few moments later clutching the locket, Anna was surprised to find Leo talking on her mobile phone which she'd left on the table.

'Here she is, Bruno, I'll hand you over,' Leo said.

'Hi,' Anna said. 'How did it go this morning? We saw the cars,' she added.

'It was a beautiful service but I still can't believe that Philippe has gone,' Bruno answered. 'Can you come into town tomorrow morning?' he continued. 'Jacques wants a meeting with both of us.'

'Why?'

'He would like to meet you again.'

'I can't really see the point,' Anna said.

'Please Anna. I think you should find the time. It's important to Jacques. Ten o'clock at the Cambones', OK?'

'I've still got things to do for tomorrow night's party,' Anna protested. 'I'm not sure I can spare the time. Wednesday would be better for me.'

'Sorry Anna, I know Jacques is leaving for Paris on Wednesday. It shouldn't take more than half an hour. I can organize a car to collect and return you if that helps?'

Anna sighed before reluctantly agreeing

and saying goodbye. She turned to look at Leo.

'Jacques Cambone wants a meeting with me and Bruno tomorrow morning. Will you come with me?'

Leo shook his head. 'No.' Anna stared at him, shocked by the determination in his voice.

He held out his hand. 'Give me the locket and I'll put it on the chain.' Leo concentrated on threading the chain through the small loop at the top of the locket, before looking up at Anna.

'It's your past — only you can deal with it. We'll face the future together but we both have to deal with the baggage from our previous lives ourselves. Of course I'll support you in any way I can, but ultimately you have to face certain things alone. May I open the locket?'

Anna nodded.

Leo was silent as he looked at the faded picture of Anna and Philippe and gently fingered the few fine strands of hair that were curled around the inside of the locket. 'Jean-Philippe's?'

Anna nodded, unable to speak as her eyes filled with unexpected tears.

'Come here,' Leo said closing the locket and holding it out to place around Anna's neck. 'And I'll do it up for you.' Pushing the clasp tightly closed, he bent his head and brushed her cheeks with his lips. 'I love you so much Anna but you must relegate these ghosts to your past where they belong.'

CHAPTER 12

Daisy pulled on her best pair of skinny-leg white jeans and a pale blue sweatshirt, and topped it off with Poppy's leather jacket she'd found hanging in the wardrobe. She and Poppy had always borrowed each others' clothes so she knew it wouldn't be a problem. Nat might have instructed her not to dress up but she still wanted to look good. Idly she wondered where they would go for a drink. Be difficult to find somewhere quiet in Cannes, that was for sure.

Nat was talking to Poppy in the kitchen when she went downstairs.

'Hi. So where are we going?'

'A brasserie on the coast road at Juan les Pins,' Nat said. 'If you're happy with the transport that is,' and he handed her a crash helmet.

Daisy laughed when she saw the Vespa scooter outside. 'Nat, you're full of surprises.'

'I've got a Harley at home but these seem to be the in thing for nipping around on down here.'

Sitting behind Nat, arms clasped tightly around him, Daisy enjoyed the ride along the bord de mer as Nat expertly waved his way through the traffic. The main Juan les Pins streets when they arrived, although less crowded than Cannes, were bustling with locals and holidaymakers enjoying themselves. Parking the scooter near the marina, Nat held Daisy's hand as they strolled back towards the resort's centre.

Passing the derelict Hotel de Provence currently concealed behind scaffolding and tarpaulin Nat said, 'I love this place. I'd love to be able to put the clock back and see it in its heyday. It must have been really something. Nice to see it being restored — even if it's being converted into yet more apartments.'

'When you're a rich and famous Hollywood scriptwriter you can buy one and pretend you're a reincarnation of Scott Fitzgerald,' Daisy teased.

Nat shook his head. 'No. I want to live in the country. I don't like towns that much. A farm up in the back country here would suit me fine. Peace and quiet for being creative. How about you? Are you a real townie?'

'Grew up on the edge of a town, with fields and a wood at the end of the garden. Poppy and I were always disappearing and building dens and having adventures. So I guess I like a mixture of both town and country but I definitely prefer old houses to modern. I'd love to do what Poppy and Dan have done. Restore something.' Daisy glanced at Nat. 'That is what apparently freaked Ben out.'

'So tell me about this Ben,' Nat said. 'Marcus said you were going to join him in Australia.'

'Marcus was wrong. We'd been together about nine months and I suggested we could find a property to renovate and suddenly he decided our relationship was crowding in on him. He wasn't ready for that kind of commitment. What he really wanted was space. Australian space.'

Daisy was quiet. 'That was six months ago. I had my first letter from him last week suggesting if I was missing him as much as he missed me, I could join him out there.'

'And are you going to? Again Marcus gave me the impression you couldn't wait to book your ticket.'

'I deliberately misled Marcus,' Daisy said quietly. 'All I was thinking of doing was going out for a holiday. See Australia and finally decide how I felt about Ben when I saw him face to face, but . . .' Daisy shook her head.

'Why didn't you mention Ben to me?'

Daisy looked at Nat. Why hadn't she told him? Was it simply a question of the right moment not showing up? Or was it because she was still flirting with the idea of her and Ben getting it together again? No, definitely not that.

'Didn't know how to. I felt a bit self-conscious telling you about an ex boyfriend when you and I had only just met. I knew I liked you but I didn't know how serious you were about me.'

'Oh I'm serious about you,' Nat said. 'Have been from day one.'

'Oh,' Daisy said. 'That's nice.' And immediately felt silly for using such an inadequate, ordinary word. It was more than nice. 'Seriously nice,' she added as Nat looked at her laughing.

'Come on, let's try one of these Italian glacés. They look "seriously nice" too!' Nat said.

Sitting at the brasserie on the beach, spoon-feeding each other with tastes of their different ice creams, Daisy began to feel that her love life was getting back on track.

Four hours later after a visit to a jazz club,

when Nat put his arms around her and kissed her goodnight, Daisy trembled. There it was again. That delicious tingling feeling that only Nat aroused in her.

CHAPTER 13

Bruno was waiting outside the Cambones' restaurant when the car dropped Anna off the next morning. The window blinds had been lowered so it was impossible to see inside. Bruno and Anna had to side-step around the heap of floral tributes still lying in the restaurant entrance.

The door was ajar and as Bruno pushed it open, a bell jangled. 'Jacques, nous sommes arrivés,' he called out, closing the door securely behind him.

'J'arrive,' and Jacques Cambone materialized out of the gloom of the bar area.

'Bonjour Anna,' he said gravely, shaking her by the hand. Anna, steeling herself for the usual cheek kissing from this man who reminded her so much of Philippe, felt her hand tremble in his.

'Thank you for coming. Please sit.' Jacques gestured towards three chairs around a table with a pot of coffee and a plate of biscuits.

Anna regarded Jacques intently as he poured coffee. Identical twins they might have been, but she'd never mistaken him for Philippe the few times she'd seen them together. For her, Philippe's charisma had simply outshone his brother's.

Now though, she found herself wondering whether Jacques was still the mirror image of Philippe. Had Philippe's hair greyed at the temples like Jacques? Had he needed reading glasses like the ones Jacques had placed on a folder in front of him? Had his eyes still crinkled when he smiled?

The stress of the last week was etched across Jacques' face as he pushed a coffee across the table to Anna. 'I'm sorry we meet again under such sad circumstances,' he said quietly. 'It is a pity you did not return to Cannes before. Philippe would have loved to see you again.'

Anna accepted the rebuke and the coffee silently, willing him to tell her what the meeting was all about.

'I've found something amongst my brother's possessions that I think by rights belongs to you. Also,' Jacques paused. 'Philippe left you some papers.' Anna stared at him as he reached into the folder and pulled out two envelopes.

One, small and brown around the edges

and bearing an old-fashioned stamp, was clearly old. Anna recognized her father's writing scrawled across the crossed out address: 'Gone Away. Return to Sender.' She fought back the tears as she realized it was Philippe's reply to the news of her pregnancy all those years ago. The envelope had never been opened.

The other, larger envelope, was new, unstamped and bare except for her name written across it. Anna's fingers trembled as she stretched out her hand to take the envelopes.

'Philippe started to write the things you'll find in there after he received the first letter,' Jacques said.

Anna bit her lip and tried to stop the tears flowing down her cheeks. Gratefully she accepted the handkerchief Bruno offered. 'I'm sorry,' she said. 'This is all so unexpected.' She looked at Jacques. 'What is happening? Can you tell me who has been in touch? Bruno did tell me it was a woman.'

'A Felicity Howell wrote on behalf of her husband who believes he is Philippe's son. She is telephoning me this afternoon,' Jacques said. 'I hope to learn more from her then.'

'Did the letter mention her husband's mother?'

Jacques shook his head. 'No. It simply said her husband had been adopted at birth and had never known either of his real parents. But when I speak with her, I will try to extract as much information from her as I can.'

'Anna,' Bruno said gently, 'there is more. Philippe's lawyer wants a meeting with you. A couple of months ago I witnessed Philippe's will — you were to be a beneficiary if you could be found at the time of his death.'

Anna stared at him. 'Me? A beneficiary?'

Bruno nodded. 'Yes Anna. The lawyer will explain when you meet him later.'

'Why don't you take the envelopes and read Philippe's letters in private and we can meet again later in the week,' Jacques suggested.

'I'll ring for the car,' Bruno said reaching for his mobile phone.

Anna stopped him. 'No don't do that Bruno. I think I'd like to take a walk. Clear my head. I'll see you tonight at the party. And Jacques, thank you. It was nice to meet you again too.'

Anna pushed her way through the crowds on the Croisette and began making her way along Quai Saint Pierre with just a single thought in her mind. She had to get away from all these people. A poster for the ferry

168

boats that operated between Cannes and the Iles de Lérins caught her eye. Running the length of Quai M. Lebeuf she bought a ticket for the next sailing and was the last person to board the crowded boat.

Twenty minutes later she followed her fellow passengers up the quay to the small traffic-free road that circled the island. Watching as everyone else took the clockwise route, Anna deliberately turned right and began making her way along the coastal track towards an almost deserted beach.

Perched on a small rock Anna finally opened the letter Philippe had sent her nearly forty years ago.

'My Darling, What wonderful news! Where shall we get married — France or England? Where shall we live while the island cottage is being done up? What shall we call the baby? Will you come to America with me? (I promise we'll be back in time for "it" to be born in France — or England, whatever you decide.) I can barely believe we're going to be a family so quickly. I promise to take the greatest care of you both. All my love, Philippe.' Underneath his signature the words 'One Life, One Love' were followed by a string of kisses.

Anna gazed out unseeingly across the Mediterranean towards Cannes, tears spilling from her eyes. Why hadn't she believed in their love more? Whatever her parents had said all those years ago about it being a 'holiday romance' with Philippe taking advantage of her naivety, had been so wrong. Philippe *had* wanted her and Jean-Philippe. The fault was all hers for not believing in him and allowing her parents to bully her into doing what they wanted and considered to be the right thing.

A family running down to chase and splash each other on the edge of the sea a few metres away from her jolted Anna out of the trance-like state she'd slipped into remembering the past. She watched them for a few moments, envying their easy familiarity with each other before pulling the contents of the second envelope out with shaking fingers.

Hesitantly Anna flipped through the pages of the spiral bound notebook dislodging a piece of folded paper that fluttered down to the shingle at her feet. Picking it up, she began to read:

'Ma Chérie, this is a letter I hope to give you when we are together again.

'I can't tell you how excited I am by the arrival of a letter about a man who could turn out to be our child. To think, after all these years I could be about to meet my son and through him, you again. I intend to keep a journal record as things unfold so that when we all finally meet, you will be able to see how everything happened. I fervently pray that this is not a false alarm and we will be able to finally welcome our son into his family.

'I appreciate how different your life must be after all these years and you may find it upsetting as the past makes its presence known in the present, but if nothing else, I hope we can meet as friends and share a part of our lives in the future.'

A simple 'Philippe' signature this time at the bottom of the page. No quotation. No kisses.

Anna re-folded the piece of paper and carefully slipped it in towards the back of the notebook as she opened it. Philippe had started his journal six weeks earlier, carefully dating the first page — the day he'd received the first letter.

Reading Philippe's journal and his obvious delight in the possibility of meeting his son, Anna could once again hear the voice of the boy she'd loved. The pages were full of his thoughts and hopes for the future. And questions about how she, Anna, would be.

'Will I recognize you — you, me? I was so

171

angry with you when you disappeared. The one thing I wanted was to find you and care for you. For years I tried to find you. Hoped you'd get in touch with me. I saw you once in the audience at the Film Institute in London but you'd left the building before I could get to you. I saw you getting into a taxi and vanishing out of my life again. The years and life took on their own momentum and suddenly twenty years had passed. I realized even if I did find you, it was too late for us to be that happy family but I couldn't — and didn't — stop looking for you. But you vanished very effectively.'

The last entry started: 'Today Jacques and I had words about me meeting my son. He is very sceptical about things working out but I believe they will. I feel in my heart of hearts that the time has finally come for me to be able to right wrongs done so many years ago. I'm off to America tomorrow, when I return the Cannes Film Festival will be in full swing — who knows, by the time it finishes I may have definite news about our family. "Our family." Oh, how I love that phrase.'

Anna, unable to control her sobbing, searched frantically for a tissue in her bag, aware that the family playing nearby were watching her, trying to hide their concern.

She forced a smile in their direction, praying they wouldn't approach her, and tried to stop herself shaking. The blue 'missed message' light on her mobile in the bottom of her bag was flashing. Leo.

With shaking fingers she pressed the redial button and waited for Leo to pick up.

'Anna, where are you? I've been frantic with worry. Bruno told me you left him hours ago.'

'I'm on Saint Marguerite. Leo darling, I'm so sorry. I just had to be by myself for a while.'

'Are you okay?' Leo asked. 'Bruno said it was an emotional meeting with Jacques.'

'It was.'

'You need to be here. Poppy needs to talk to you about finalizing things for this evening. There still seems a lot to be done.'

'I'll be back soon. I promise I'll catch the next boat back. There's one coming across the bay now. Leo, we need to talk when I get back.'

'We'll talk all you like after this party is out of the way,' Leo said firmly. 'There are things I need to say as well. I'll tell Poppy you'll be here within the hour then.'

Thoughtfully Anna closed her phone. Carefully she placed the two envelopes with their revealing contents in her bag. She had

173

all the proof she'd ever needed that Philippe Cambone had truly loved her — had probably still loved her at the time of his death.

Anna pressed her hands against her eyes and rubbed hard, trying yet again to stem the tears. She knew she had only herself to blame for the mess she'd made of things. But how was she going to live with herself now, knowing how much she'd hurt Philippe with her selfish act of giving their son away?

CHAPTER 14

'So how was your evening with Nat? Heard you come in at two,' Poppy said as she and Daisy did some last minute party food shopping in Forville market. 'Did you tell Nat about Ben?'

'Oh, hope I didn't wake you. It was a great night. Nat and I seem to be on the same wavelength over lots of things. He took me to a jazz club he knew up in Valbonne after Juan les Pins. He actually likes Jamie Callum as well. Remember how Ben always used to moan at me for listening to him? And yes, I told him all about Ben.' Daisy looked at her sister.

'Can you believe Marcus had also poked his oar in? Gave Nat the impression that I couldn't wait to jet off to be reunited with him. At least you didn't do that. Two dozen eggs enough?'

'Plenty. Cheese counter next. And how did he react?'

'He was fine — told me all about Julia the love of his life in primary school,' Daisy laughed. She'd really enjoyed last night. Nat was so good to be around. He thought her plans for the future — going freelance and moving into the cottage were great. But did she have the courage to go it alone? Even if Nat was a part of her life?

As Poppy agonized over how big a Brie to buy and whether Gorgonzola was a popular choice, or should she just stick with Stilton, Daisy wandered over to the flower section to look at several vases filled with one of her favourites — vibrant, happy sunflowers. Just what she needed — a visual reminder of the happy mood she was in. Her mobile trilled its text alert as she selected three sunflowers and paid for them.

'Seen any reasonable asparagus anywhere?' Poppy asked, joining her.

'That stall over there. And the next one for the olives and the tapenade you wanted. Think that's everything on the list then. No, we still need some smoked salmon.'

Walking back to the car with Poppy, Daisy took a quick look to see who the text was from. She didn't recognize the international number and it wasn't until they'd stowed the shopping in the car and were driving home that she clicked on the message.

'srry hve bn fool. rtrning to uk nxt wk 2 marry u. lv u. ben.'

Daisy hit her knees with her fist clenched.

'I don't believe this,' she said reading the message out to Poppy. 'Now what do I do?' she said.

'You should have replied to his letter telling him it was too late, days ago,' Poppy said, with a typical bossy big sister tone to her voice. 'You'll have to text him back and tell him no way.'

'Isn't it typical of Ben though to assume I've nothing better to do than hang around waiting for him.' Daisy threw the phone in her bag.

'Aren't you going to text him right away?' Poppy asked.

'No. I'll e-mail him the minute we get back,' Daisy said. 'I'm not that keen on texts. All those abbreviated words can lead to misunderstandings. I'm going to have to spell it out in full. Make sure he gets the message. Can't you drive a bit faster? I need to get this over and done with.'

'No, it's a thirty speed limit along here. I don't want a speeding ticket, thank you very much. What are you going to say?'

'That if he thinks he can just waltz back into my life and nothing will have changed, then he's not only wrong but stupid. Besides

I won't be in the UK next week.'

Once back at the cottage sitting in front of her laptop, Daisy clicked on Ben's e-mail address. Thank God she hadn't deleted it from her address book in a fit of pique. Now, how to be polite and firm but kind?

'Dear Ben, re your recent text. Marriage is not on, I'm afraid, so suggest you stay where you are. Am out of the UK next week. Have a good life. Daisy.'

Thoughtfully she looked at what she'd written. Too short? Too cruel? But what else was there to say? She didn't want him harbouring any false hopes of a reconciliation. This last week since she'd met Nat had convinced her there was absolutely no way she wanted Ben back in her life. Ben was in the past — his choice. Nat was the future — her choice.

'P.S. Hope you meet someone special soon. I have and I'm very happy.'

There, that should get the message across. Daisy pressed the send button before she could change her mind. Her computer pinged. Incoming mail — one from the paper, two from journalist friends. Daisy read them in a daze before closing her laptop. That was all she needed.

Poppy glanced at her as she walked into the sitting-room. 'Told him? Good. You all right? You look a bit dazed.'

'I've been sacked as of the end of the Festival. Bill the editor has gone already and rumour has it at least ten per cent of the staff face the chop.'

'Can they do that?'

Daisy nodded. 'Short term contracts aren't being renewed. Marcus is fired as well,' Daisy said. 'Oh well, I suppose it's an ill wind. At least I'll get some redundancy money to kick start my freelancing with. Think I might be living down here sooner than I expected.'

'Fine by me,' Poppy said. 'Now, can we get on with the party preparations?'

CHAPTER 15

Anna could see Leo waiting for her on the quay as the ferryboat pulled alongside the pontoon. The last to step ashore, Anna ran towards Leo, a feeling of relief washing over her as he put his arms around her and held her tightly for several seconds without speaking.

'Are you all right?' he asked finally, holding her at arms length and studying her face. 'I was so worried when you didn't return.'

'I'm sorry Leo. I just needed to be on my own to read the papers Jacques and Bruno gave me. And to think about what they had said.'

Leo looked at Anna questioningly as he noticed the envelopes sticking out of her bag for the first time.

'I'll tell you what happened this morning as we walk back to the villa,' Anna said. She tucked her hand into Leo's.

'Preparations going okay for the party?'

Leo nodded. 'Think Poppy is getting stressed having to take decisions she feels you should be making but other than that, things are on schedule for this evening.'

'Good,' Anna answered. 'Although I've never felt less like a party in my life,' she added quietly.

Walking along the bord de mer Anna told Leo the name of the woman who had contacted Philippe. 'Felicity Howell. Which means nothing to Jacques, Bruno or me.'

She also told him about the long lost letter from Philippe and the journal that Jacques had given her.

'I wish I'd come back to Cannes years ago and found Philippe. Told him the truth. My life could have been so different. So much better.' She sighed. 'Still it's too late now.'

Leo was silent and Anna glanced at him, concerned. She'd clearly upset him today, first by disappearing and now by inferring how much better her life would have been if she'd married Philippe all those years ago. Anna bit her lip. The last thing she wanted to do was hurt Leo. She loved him too much.

'I don't think you coming to Cannes this year was a very good idea,' Leo said slowly. 'You seem to have jumped on to an emotional roller coaster that is in danger of running you over. I dread to think what would have happened if Philippe had been here in person.'

Leo indicated an empty bench overlooking the beach and the Mediterranean. 'Let's sit down for a few moments. I need to say something to you. I don't think it can wait until after the party like I thought, after all.'

Obediently Anna followed Leo across to the bench and sat down. As Leo took her hand in his, Anna's engagement ring glinted in the rays from the overhead sun. Leo gently fingered the ring before starting to speak.

'I'm beginning to wonder if Philippe hadn't died and the two of you had met up again this week, whether you and I would be preparing to announce our engagement tonight.' He was silent for a moment, gazing out to sea before turning to face her. 'This pining for something that might have been has to stop, Anna, if we are to have any sort of future.' His hand holding hers squeezed so hard Anna thought her fingers would drop off.

'We are both old enough to know, and accept, that nothing is ever simply black or white — particularly with the baggage we all collect as we go through life. By the time we get to our age,' Leo shrugged. 'Well, there's usually lots of it.' He was silent for a second or two before continuing.

'Anna, we have to be totally honest with each other before our relationship can go any further. I love you with all my heart — I feel we're soulmates. But I'm scared I'm only second best for you after Philippe. I'm worried too that there is always going to be a dead presence in our marriage. A presence that won't allow me to get as close to you as I want to. I truly couldn't bear that.'

Anna stared out across the bay knowing that whatever she said to Leo in the future, nothing would ever be more important than what she said this minute.

'Leo, you must never ever think again you're second best in my life. The time I've known you has been the happiest of my adult life. I didn't expect to ever love and be loved in return — I thought it was far too late. But I do love you, Leo, and I can't imagine my life without you in it.' Anna paused. 'What you said about us being soulmates is true. I'm sorry about inflicting my pain over the past and Philippe on to you. I don't want a dead presence in our marriage, any more than you do. But it's Philippe's legacy that is at stake here.' Her hand still rested in Leo's, clenched into a fist. 'It's the possibility of finally meeting my son, Jean-Philippe, that is really beginning to tear me apart in all this.'

Anna turned to face Leo, her voice taking on a desperate note. 'You've got children. Imagine if you no longer had any contact with Alison. If there was a possibility you would never see your grandchild. How would you feel? I know the whole sorry business is my fault — I was the one who denied Philippe his rights as a father when I gave Jean-Philippe away — but now if there's just a chance I can explain things to the next generation, make amends in some way, then I have to try. Please help me to get through this Leo.'

'Anna, it's impossible to know what Philippe's true feelings were for you all those years ago. Or whether things would have worked out if you and he had stayed together. As for Jean-Philippe,' Leo shook his head. 'Who knows what kind of effect finding him will have on your — on our — lives?

'I promise I'll give you all the help I can but when will all this torment stop? When we leave here at the end of the week? Or will you carry on punishing yourself for the past? Beating yourself up with guilt?'

Anna handed him the letter Philippe had written. 'No, it's not impossible to know what Philippe's true feelings were. Read this and then tell me I shouldn't feel guilty about things.'

She stared at Leo's impassive face as he read the letter, trying to gauge his reaction to the emotions expressed by Philippe so long ago.

'Now do you see why I can't give up this emotional roller coaster as you called it, until I have some sort of closure over my past?' she asked quietly as Leo handed back the letter.

He nodded. 'But I still think you're wrong to take one hundred percent of the blame on your shoulders. There were other people involved all along the line.'

'I know,' Anna said. 'But I'm the last one left who can try to right the mistakes that were made.'

Leo sighed. 'L.P. Hartley was right when he said the past is a foreign country. It's certainly not a place I'm keen to visit for long. I just want us to get back on track to enjoying the rest of our lives together.'

'We will, I promise. I'm looking forward to the future with you so much,' Anna said. 'But there's something else you have to know.'

Leo looked at her warily and waited for her to continue.

'Philippe has named me as a beneficiary in his will. I have to meet his lawyers soon for them to tell me what that means exactly. Will you come with me this time please, Leo?'

'Yes, but I need you to promise me one thing, Anna. Whatever happens, whatever you inherit, please don't let it come between us and destroy what we have *now* in the present.'

'I promise,' Anna said, and oblivious to passers-by, leant forward and kissed Leo passionately.

CHAPTER 16

'I picked up a sparkling candle too,' Daisy said as she and Poppy admired the iced gateau with its swirls of cream and chocolate hearts Daisy had collected from the patisserie. 'I thought it would go well . . . here,' and she carefully pushed it into the centre of the cake. 'We can light it just before Leo makes his announcement.'

'Better put the cake in the fridge,' Poppy said. 'Don't want the cream going off before tonight.'

'Right,' Daisy said. 'Now where's that list? What have we got left to do?'

Poppy looked at her clipboard. 'Think we're done. We just have to put the food out on the table what, quarter of an hour before people are due?' she said glancing at her watch. 'We'll have to light the candles and float them on the pool but that's not until later as well. Nat will be bringing Tom back soon. Shall we eat something with him or wait for food this evening?'

'Oh let's eat something light with Tom. Shouldn't drink champagne on an empty stomach,' Daisy said.

'Anna and Leo look as if they are still putting the world to rights,' Daisy added, looking across to the villa where Anna and Leo were sitting by the pool. 'Anna's looking pretty miserable too. I wonder what's upset her? Tonight's supposed to be a happy occasion.'

'I thought she looked as if she'd been crying when they got back here earlier,' Poppy said. 'She was very subdued when I went across to ask what time they were planning to make the formal announcement of their engagement. I need to know for bringing the champagne out for the toast,' Poppy explained. 'Leo said he'd let me know later.' She shrugged. 'Hope he doesn't forget.'

She turned as Nat opened the garden gate. 'Ah, Tom and Cindy are back. I'll organize some food. Would you and Cindy like to stay?' she asked Nat.

'Thanks. Not sure how hungry these two will be. Lots of candy-floss and other delicacies on offer today on the Croisette — along with balloons,' he said, catching hold of Cindy's pink helium filled balloon as it threatened to slip out of the little girl's hand

and float away from her. Daisy helped Tom tie his blue one to the back of a chair before following Poppy into the kitchen to fetch the food.

'How's your day been then?' Nat asked as Daisy put packets of crisps on the table for the children.

'Apart from losing my job? I'm out of work as from this Sunday,' she explained as Nat looked at her. 'Looks like I'm going to be freelance sooner rather than later.'

'Which you can do from anywhere in the world,' Nat said thoughtfully.

'True but first I'll need to do some serious networking to let people know I'm available. Poppy's already agreed I can have the cottage while I look around for something down here.'

'A new start in all sorts of ways,' Nat said. 'Exciting.'

'Yep,' Daisy said, deciding not to mention the other event in her day, Ben's marriage proposal. She'd tell him later of course, when they could laugh about it together.

'Cindy, Tom, I'm going to make you chocolate milkshakes. OK?'

Half an hour later the children finished their tea and Nat pushed his chair back. 'Time to go, Cindy,' he said.

As they said their goodbyes and untied

Cindy's balloon, Anna walked through the villa garden towards the cottage.

'Hello Tom and Cindy. Love your balloons.'

'Are you having balloons for your party?' Cindy asked.

'No, we completely forgot about ordering balloons,' Anna said.

'That's sad,' Cindy said. 'You can borrow mine if you like,' she offered holding it out to Anna. 'Not to keep. Just for your party.'

'Thank you Cindy. That's very kind of you,' Anna said. 'It's your birthday tomorrow isn't it?' she asked. 'You'll need your balloon for your tea party then, so better take it home with you now.'

'Okay,' Cindy said. 'Is my mummy coming to your party?'

'She's welcome to come but I expect she's busy with Festival things. I think Nat's coming,' Anna said, glancing across at him.

'Mummy's not busy. I heard her telling Daddy she didn't have anything to do tonight.'

'Well you tell her if she wants to come with Nat, she'll be very welcome,' Anna said. 'It would be nice to meet her.'

'Come on Cindy, let's go,' Nat said. 'I'll see you all later.'

'Bye Cindy, have a lovely birthday tomorrow. Such a sweet little girl,' Anna said before turning to Poppy.

'Leo suggests about quarter to nine for the champagne and cake. Everyone should be here by then and afterwards we can just party.'

'OK, Daisy and I will bring it out then,' Poppy said. 'And now we'd all better think about getting ready.'

The sun had set over the Esterel mountains to the right of the villa as Daisy lit the floating candles and pushed them out on to the still water of the swimming-pool. Poppy was lighting the extra torch candles in their bamboo holders she'd placed on the driveway and Leo was dealing with the lantern candles around the villa. The gentle strains of a Cole Porter song as the pianist began his warm-up medley were drifting around the garden competing with the noise of the resident frogs.

Anna, in the kitchen to collect a tray of glasses, watched all the last minute activity and smiled to herself. The villa garden in the twilight with all the candles was looking romantic. She knew Leo was looking forward to announcing their engagement later. Despite the uncertainty shrouding her past, life at this moment was good and promising to get even better with Leo at her side permanently from now on. The future was what truly mattered, not the secrets of the past.

'I think we should make a toast to Poppy and Daisy,' Anna said as Leo handed her a glass of champagne a few moments later. 'You've both worked so hard. Everything looks wonderful. Thank you. Oh, here comes Rick,' she said, turning to greet her business partner.

'And Marcus has arrived too,' Daisy said. 'With a friend. Excuse me a moment,' and she made her way over to Marcus as his blonde companion went to look at the buffet table.

'What's she doing here? Anna didn't invite her.'

'Everybody gate crashes parties down here. You should have security on the gates checking tickets if you want to avoid unwanted guests.'

'It's not that sort of party,' Daisy said. 'And you're not a guest — you're the official photographer.'

'So, she's my assistant.' Marcus shrugged.

'Go and take some photos then and make sure your "assistant" doesn't get in the way,' Daisy said. 'I'm going to go and apologize to Anna about your uninvited guest.'

Several other people arrived at that moment and Daisy, seeing Anna busy making introductions, decided to leave her apology until later making her way instead over to Poppy who was counting glasses on a side table near the buffet.

'I hope we don't run out of glasses,' Poppy said. 'D'you think everyone is here yet?'

'Anna said she expected about forty, didn't she?' Daisy said, looking around and trying to do a rough head count. 'So, yes, I think most people are here. Nat isn't though. Hope he gets here before the food disappears.' And Daisy helped herself to a plate of appetisers from the buffet.

'Seen any one famous yet?' she asked, offering Poppy a smoked salmon blini. 'Try one. I know the cook. They're delicious.'

'Thanks. No, don't recognize a single face. No, I lie,' Poppy said. 'The handsome man who's just arrived with a blonde and another man, looks very much like your Nat. Don't know who the couple are though.'

Daisy turned to look down the driveway. 'Poppy, how can you not recognize Verity Raymond? Cindy obviously told her what Anna said about her being welcome to come. And the guy is Bruno. A big shot down here in film world on the money side of things.'

The two watched as Anna greeted Bruno like an old friend and then welcomed Verity to the party, before introducing them both to Leo.

'That's interesting,' Daisy said quietly. 'Bruno was a great friend of Philippe Cambone. I wonder if Anna knew him as well back in the past. I must ask her.'

Poppy looked at her sister anxiously. 'Please, don't start asking questions tonight. Let Anna enjoy her engagement party. I think the last few days have been very hard on her for some reason. She's been very subdued every time I've seen her.'

'Poppy, what d'you take me for? Of course I won't bother Anna tonight. Might have a word with Bruno though,' Daisy said mischievously, ignoring Poppy's sharp intake of breath and smiling at Nat making his way towards them.

'Nat. You're late. Everything OK?' Daisy asked as Nat hugged and kissed her.

'Think so. Verity and Teddy had a major fallout earlier. That's why we're late. To be honest, I'm surprised Verity still wanted to come but she said she needed to get out of the villa. And she wanted to meet Anna. Thanks,' he said, accepting a glass of champagne from a passing waitress.

'Love your headband. Very flapperish. You

look lovely,' he said gently kissing Daisy again and placing an arm around her shoulder. 'Dance with me later?'

'Of course. Not sure I'm up to the Charleston though,' Daisy said, watching a couple by the pool giving it their best as the pianist romped through 'Aint She Sweet'. 'It always looks so complicated to me. All that leg swinging and knee holding.'

'Don't worry. It's one of the few dances I can do,' Nat said. 'In fact I'm a bit of an expert. My gran was a great rag-time dancer and taught me everything she knew.'

'Daisy, I think Leo is about to make the announcement,' Poppy interrupted. 'We'd better get the cake and have the extra champagne at the ready.'

'Back in five,' Daisy said, handing Nat her champagne glass. 'Ready for the toast.'

'I'll keep this short,' Leo said, calling for everyone's attention. 'Some of you know already that this isn't just another Festival de Cannes party but for those of you who are unaware, we have two reasons for celebration tonight. *Future Promises* was well received at the festival and we raise our glasses to Helen and Rupert — stars of the future.'

He paused as Helen and Rupert acknowledged the cheers and the applause. 'The other, personal, reason for celebration,' Leo continued, 'is that Anna has done me the honour of agreeing to become my wife.'

As everyone shouted congratulations and Daisy carried the cake out with its sparkling candle, Leo took Anna into his arms. 'All I want to say Anna my darling, is that I love you and will do my utmost to make you happy for the rest of our lives.'

The gentle strains of 'Come Fly With Me' floated on the evening air as the happy couple swayed gently together and everyone raised their glasses. 'Anna and Leo.'

CHAPTER 17

An hour or so later when the party was in full swing, and Leo and Rick were deep in discussion about the woes of both the publishing and film worlds, Anna slipped away for a few moments by herself.

So many people here wishing her and Leo well; some she knew as friends, others she knew as business acquaintances, others she had no idea who they were. She could see Bruno on the terrace standing apart from everyone and taking a call on his mobile. She hoped she'd get the opportunity to talk to him before the evening finished. See if he had any idea what Philippe had written in his will before she went to the lawyers tomorrow.

There was somebody sitting on the upholstered swing seat hidden away in a quiet corner at the top of the garden. Not wanting company, Anna was about to turn and leave when she heard the sound of sobbing.

Moving closer she asked quietly. 'Are you all right? Can I help? Or would you rather be left alone?'

The tear-stained face that Verity Raymond turned towards her made her hurry forward, and sitting alongside her she gently placed an arm around Verity's shoulders and waited for the younger woman to compose herself.

'Teddy is furious with me,' Verity said struggling to control her sobs. 'He thought I'd given up on something, but today when I told him some exciting news, he realized I hadn't. He's even accused me of trying to get my own way by deceit and going behind his back. He was still on about it this evening and we had another major row.' Verity wiped her face with the back of her hand.

'All I want is for him to be happy and for us to have another baby. He adores Cindy and I'm sure he'd feel the same about another child but now he just refuses to discuss it.'

'Cindy is a delightful child,' Anna said. 'You must be so proud of her.'

'Yes. I am. But I do worry that she is being spoilt as an only child. I had been hoping she would have some brothers or sisters before now but,' Verity shook her head. 'Anyway, I mustn't bore you with my personal problems. What are you doing up here? It's your party going on down there. You should be down there living it up.'

'Oh I just needed some time out,' Anna said. 'You know how it is.'

Verity nodded her agreement. 'Maybe this is the wrong moment but I was hoping to talk to you sometime about your new film project. Would there be a part for me in the film?'

Anna looked at her astonished. 'But it's a period drama. Not your sort of thing surely?'

'My very first role in rep was Rosalie the maid in *Lady Windermere's Fan*. I've had a soft spot for costume drama ever since. The contemporary stuff I do now is great fun but I'd love a chance to wear long skirts for a change!'

'Well, I'll tell the casting director about your interest but I can't promise anything,' Anna said. 'You know shooting is going to start this autumn in the UK? Don't you live in the States these days?'

'We're buying a place near my parents in Gloucestershire. Cindy needs to be settled in school for the next few years,' Verity said. 'At least Teddy and I are agreed on that, and that it will be in England.'

'Well, when you're settled in Gloucestershire we'll meet up. I'm, well Leo actually, is quite close, in the Cotswolds, and when we're married I'll be moving there. You must come for lunch and we'll get to know each other properly.'

'I'd like that. Thank you Anna.'

'Ah, this is where you're hiding,' Leo said, suddenly appearing at the top of the path. 'Anna darling, Bruno has been looking for you. He wanted to talk to you before he left. You may just catch him if you're quick. If not, you're to phone him tomorrow.'

'I was hoping to have a word with him too. Excuse me, Verity. I'll see you later.' Anna made her way back down into the garden and on to the driveway where she could see Bruno standing by the villa gates.

'Bruno, you're not leaving already? Leo says you were looking for me?'

'Yes. I have something to tell you.'

'Something about Philippe?'

'Jacques phoned an hour ago to tell me about the telephone conversations he's had with Felicity Howell.' Bruno looked at Anna before saying quietly.

'Anna, I think I already know the answer to my question, but I'd really appreciate you telling me the truth yourself. Did you . . .'

'Yes,' Anna interrupted. 'I had Philippe Cambone's baby. I named him Jean-

Philippe. And then I gave him away.'

'I thought so,' Bruno said. 'Oh Anna. I don't know what to say.'

'Nothing to say,' Anna said quietly. 'Other than for me to say I'm sorry Philippe never got a chance to meet his son.'

'Yes, he would have welcomed that,' Bruno said. 'Jacques has also been putting two and two together by the way. He asked Felicity if she knew the name of her husband's mother. She said yes, it was on the copy of the original birth certificate they'd managed to obtain, but that it was proving impossible to trace her.'

Bruno glanced at Anna. 'Rightly or wrongly, when she told him the name, Jacques said he knew a woman with that name and that she was in town for the festival. Felicity immediately begged him to arrange a private meeting for her and her husband.'

Anna gasped. 'What did Jacques say?'

'That it wasn't his decision but he would see if he could arrange a meeting. He's asked me to talk to you first because it's not as straightforward as it seems,' Bruno paused.

'Her husband has had second thoughts about this whole business of tracing his roots. Because Philippe died before they

201

could meet up he has decided not to continue the search for his mother.' Bruno was silent for a moment. 'Basically because he's very bitter about the fact that she gave him up. So even if you agree to a meeting, there's no guarantee that he will come. It could turn out to be just you and this Felicity Howell.'

'Is her husband in town for the festival too? Do we know what he does?' Anna asked.

'Yes he's in town. And he has some sort of connection with the film industry. Felicity was vague on the subject — deliberately, Jacques felt. Will you let Jacques arrange a meeting?'

'I don't know,' Anna said with a sigh. 'Is there any point if my son has decided he doesn't want to see me? Doesn't want to have any contact because I abandoned him?'

'But wouldn't you like to know about his life? Learn how he's turned out? There are all sorts of things his wife could tell you. Maybe even persuade her husband to meet after all.'

'Have you met this Felicity woman? What is she like?'

Bruno shook his head. 'I don't know. Like Jacques I haven't met her. But she sounds genuine. Jacques says she's desperate to help her husband come to terms with his adoption. Philippe dying so close to their planned first meeting has really shaken him. He had so many questions he wanted to ask him. Questions only you can answer now. If you do meet Felicity, it might be the start of getting him to change his mind over you,' Bruno added gently.

'So you think I should agree to meet this woman?'

Bruno sighed. 'Anna, it has to be your decision and yours alone. No one is going to pressurize you into doing something you're not comfortable with.'

'I told Leo earlier that I had to continue trying to trace Jean-Philippe. But I also promised him that I would stop beating myself up with guilt. That the future was more important to me now than the past,' Anna said slowly. 'To be so close to meeting Jean-Philippe, only to learn that he despises me,' her voice trailed away. 'I don't think I could cope with him saying that to my face. Maybe it would be better just to leave things the way they are and get on with my life with Leo.'

'It's your decision, Anna,' Bruno said. 'But don't decide anything you might regret while you're so emotional. Talk it over with Leo. Sleep on it. Give me a ring when you know what you want to do. Ah, here's my taxi — and here's Leo to claim his fiancée for the last dance of the party. Goodnight Anna.'

'What did Bruno want?'

Anna, tense in Leo's arms as they danced slowly together as the notes of 'Begin the Beguine' drifted around the garden, stumbled over her own feet at his question and Leo's arms tightened around her.

'Are you okay?'

Anna shook her head. 'Not really. Can we find a quiet spot and talk?'

Wordlessly Leo led her to a deserted corner of the garden out of sight of the remaining partygoers. 'Now tell me.'

'Felicity Howell wants to meet me, even though her husband has decided he doesn't want to continue the search for his real mother.'

'Why and how does this woman know about you?' Leo demanded. 'Did Jacques tell her who you were?'

'No. It was only after Felicity told him the name on the birth certificate they'd seen was Lucinda Ann Carstairs, that he said he knew someone of that name, and that I was in town for the festival.'

'But your name isn't Lucinda Ann

Carstairs so why did he say . . .' Leo's voice died away. 'Of course. Changing your name was one of those precautions you took to ensure you disappeared wasn't it?'

'Yes. I did it all legally but my parents insisted that Lucinda Ann Carstairs died the day I gave Jean-Philippe up for adoption. Put the father's name on the certificate — he can deal with it if the boy wants to trace him in the future. But you, you change yours and disappear. Those were the instructions from my parents. They couldn't cope with the shame of a daughter who'd "gone bad". As for acknowledging an illegitimate grandson . . .' Anna was silent for a moment before continuing. 'So, I became Anna Carson; new name, new beginning. But old memories,' she said, biting her bottom lip and starting to shake.

Leo held her close and waited.

'But now, the worst part is, this Felicity says her husband despises his mother for giving him up. And has decided against continuing to try and find her. Says knowing who his father was will be enough.'

'So right now, we're talking about the possibility of you learning your son's identity, meeting his wife but not actually getting to see Jean-Philippe face to face,' Leo said slowly.

Anna nodded. 'I've got to decide whether to meet Felicity and hope her husband comes with her. Or whether to walk away — and this time it really would be forever.' She sighed.

'I don't know what to do. Bruno said I shouldn't rush into a decision about arranging a meeting, that I should sleep on it and talk it over with you.'

'I agree with Bruno. Sleep on it and tomorrow we'll talk and decide what's the best thing for you to do,' Leo said gently. 'Right now I think we should find Poppy and Daisy and say goodnight.'

Poppy and Daisy were at the table on the villa's terrace, enjoying a last glass of champagne and some of the leftover party food. Nat, who'd been wandering around the garden making sure all the candles were safely out, had just joined them.

'Hi,' Daisy said. 'It was a great party wasn't it? Are you going to join us for a late snack too?'

'We really came to say thank you for all your hard work and to say goodnight but I'd love a extra slice of quiche,' Anna said, suddenly feeling hungry. 'Need something to soak up all the champagne.'

'And I can't resist another slice of this wonderful gateau,' Leo said. 'Thanks Poppy,

Daisy. We'll always remember the evening we got engaged, won't we, Anna?'

Anna smiled. 'Definitely. Everybody seemed to enjoy themselves. Must say, you do a good Charleston, Nat.'

'Thanks. Bruno's rock and roll routine was pretty spectacular too, wasn't it?'

'He's certainly perfected it from his original attempts,' Anna laughed.

'You've known Bruno a long time then?' Daisy said, ignoring the warning look Poppy threw at her.

'Yes we go way back, but we hadn't met for years until this week,' Anna said. 'As Philippe Cambone's life-long friend he's trying to help the family sort Philippe's affairs. His unexpected death has created several problems.'

She paused slightly before continuing. 'The main one concerns his estate. Right now Bruno's involved in trying to untangle something complicated with a woman called Felicity Howell.'

'Felicity Howell?' Nat repeated.

'Yes do you know her?' Anna asked turning to him. 'She's written to the Cambones saying she believes her husband is Philippe's illegitimate child.'

'You mean there really is an illegitimate son around? It wasn't just a publicity stunt dreamt up by that actor Sean somebody or other,' Daisy said.

'Yes there really is a son and heir,' Anna said, but before she could say any more Leo stood up.

'Come on Anna, soon to be Mrs Hunter, I think it's time we said goodnight.'

'I'm going too,' Nat said, pushing his plate away and standing up.

'I'll come and open the gate for you,' Daisy said.

'Thanks for a great party, Anna — and the introductions.'

'Nat, before you go, you didn't say whether you knew this Felicity Howell,' Anna said.

Nat looked at Anna and hesitated slightly before answering. 'Yes I know a Felicity Howell — and so do you.'

Anna gave him a surprised look. 'I do?'

'Yes. She was here this evening.'

Anna looked at him in open-mouthed astonishment.

'Whether it's the same person who has contacted the Cambones I don't know,' Nat continued. 'But I do know Verity Raymond is a stage name. Her real name is Felicity Wickham — née Howell.'

Leo was just in time to catch Anna from hitting the ground as she fainted.

CHAPTER 18

'Last night I went to a private party that could have come straight out of a nostalgic 1920s film being shown here at the festival.

'Picture the idyllic setting: the candle-lit garden of a belle époque villa, piano jazz drifting on the night air, the champagne flowing into crystal glasses, handsome men flirting with elegant, beautiful women.

'An engagement is announced, people are dancing, then somebody's real name, as opposed to their stage name, is mentioned and the newly engaged heroine of the story faints. Throw in an illegitimate child, an unhappy mother, a dead father and you have a storyline fit for the next blockbuster.'

Daisy pressed the save button and sat back in her chair under the loggia. Waking early, she'd crept downstairs with her laptop to start writing her daily report.

The table was still littered with debris from the previous evening: screwed up paper napkins, discarded cocktail sticks, paper plates. Making a space for her laptop, Daisy had glanced up at the villa. The bedroom curtains were still drawn and downstairs the kitchen blind was pulled.

As Anna had regained consciousness after fainting last night, Leo had taken charge saying, 'I think the best thing for Anna is bed,' and wishing everyone goodnight, he'd gently led Anna into the villa and closed the door behind them.

'Oh dear,' Poppy had said. 'I do hope Anna is okay. Hasn't got food poisoning or anything. I'd hate to think I was responsible for making anyone ill.'

'You are such an old worrier, sis,' Daisy said. 'I think Anna just had a shock that's all.'

Afterwards, when Nat had left, Daisy helped Poppy to take the leftover food into the kitchen before they went to bed. 'Leave everything else,' Poppy had said, smothering a yawn. 'I'll throw all the rubbish into a bin bag tomorrow.'

'Morning Daisy,' Poppy said now, appearing with two mugs of coffee and a plate of croissants, 'couldn't you sleep either?'

'No. Thought I'd try and get ahead with today's report. I've promised Nat I'll meet up with him later in Cannes, so I need to get organized. No sign of life over there yet,' Poppy said, looking across at the villa.

'Wonder how Anna is this morning? I'll go across later and see if Leo thinks she needs a doctor to check her over. Fainting like that for no reason,' Poppy shook her head.

'Come on sis,' Daisy said. 'Even you must be starting to put two and two together about Anna's past.'

'What d'you mean?'

Daisy tapped her fingers. 'One: Anna comes to the Festival for the first time in years. Two: Philippe Cambone, an international film director who she initially denies knowing, dies unexpectedly. Three: there's a rumour circulating of an illegitimate heir making a claim against the film director's estate. Four: A woman using an alias to contact the Cambones about the said illegitimate heir, turns out to be married to the up-and-coming producer, Teddy Wickham. Five —'

'Stop,' Poppy said. 'So are you suggesting Anna is somehow involved in all this?'

'I think she's right at the centre of things. I'm ninety-nine percent certain she'll turn out to be Teddy Wickham's mother,' Daisy said.

■ ■ ■ ■

Anna pulled her croissant apart and pushed the pile of crumbs around her plate.

'You were meant to eat that, not play with it,' Leo said.

'Not really hungry,' Anna said. 'Sorry.'

She glanced across at Leo. 'What time are we going down into Cannes today? I can't remember.'

'Your appointment with the lawyer is for eleven,' Leo said.

'I want to get Cindy a birthday present,' Anna said. 'A proper present from her long-lost grandmother.'

A short silence followed her words before Leo sighed. 'Oh Anna darling. You don't think you're leaping to conclusions too soon here? You haven't got one hundred percent confirmation yet that Teddy Wickham is going to turn out to be your Jean-Philippe. Or that he will even agree to meet you.'

'I know, I know. But the more I think about it, the more certain I am that he is my Jean-Philippe. Anyway, I'm going to buy Cindy something special for her birthday,' Anna said stubbornly. 'From a friend. She did offer me her pink balloon for the party. It's the least I can do.'

'And Teddy and Verity? Are you going to meet them now? Discuss the possibility of your relationship? Tell them who you are? Or rather who you used to be?'

Anna shook her head. 'Tell them I was Lucinda Ann Carstairs in another life? No. If Teddy is really going to give up searching for his mother there is no point at the moment. But I shall keep in touch with Verity and Cindy as me, Anna Carson.' She looked at Leo anticipating his reaction. 'Did you know they are planning to move to England? To Gloucestershire. We'll virtually be neighbours when we're married. We can meet up with them as Mr and Mrs Hunter.'

'Let me get this straight. You're planning to become friends with Verity and her family without telling them the truth about your relationship to Teddy and Cindy? Why?'

'Because if Teddy hates his mother that much for giving him away and he learns my true identity, he could stop Verity and Cindy from seeing me,' Anna said. 'I'll become a good friend to them all before I think about telling them the truth.'

'Oh, so, you do plan on telling them someday?'

'Yes, when Teddy knows and trusts me.'

'He'd never trust you again, if you do this, believe me.' Leo ran his hands through his hair. 'Anna, this is so not a good thing to do. Please think about it.'

'I can't stop thinking about it, Leo,' Anna said. 'How else can I stay in touch with Cindy? Watch her grow up?'

'I don't know,' Leo said. 'But I do know that by getting the truth out into the open and not compounding past mistakes you stand a far better chance of living happily in the future.'

Anna slumped down into her chair. 'Leo, I'm frightened telling the truth will make everything go wrong again and I'll never get to know Cindy, my grandchild, properly, or Teddy.'

Leo took her left hand in his and squeezed it. 'Anna, even if you're terrified about the outcome, I really urge you to tell Verity and Teddy who you are. You could write a letter if you don't want to tell them face to face but I feel having come this far, you need to see things through to the truthful end.'

Anna bit her lip as Leo continued. 'Think about it, Anna. You didn't come to Cannes this year looking for your long-lost son. You came simply hoping to finally tell Philippe the truth. To tell him that somewhere in the world was a son he'd never met. The fact that Philippe died before you could make your confession, has just complicated things.'

'What do you mean?'

'Instead of telling Philippe about his son, you have to tell the son about his father.'

Thoughtfully Leo brushed her face with a finger. 'Teddy deserves to know the truth about his birth and adoption, and about how much you loved his father. Meet Verity, tell her your story, please. She can at least talk to Teddy and he can then decide whether he wants to acknowledge you or not. And I suppose what I'm really saying Anna is this: you've lived all your adult life without either Philippe or your son. You know you can survive with neither of them in your life, but the truth still needs to be told. Then you and I can get on with the rest of our lives together.'

There was a serious look in his eyes as he said, 'Promise me you'll think seriously about meeting Verity.'

Before she could answer, Anna's mobile phone rang and Leo watched as she quickly snatched it up.

'Oh hello.' Anna listened for a moment.

'I'll mention it to Leo but I doubt we'll come, Bruno. I think I've had enough of parties for a while. Thanks for calling. Speak later,' and she ended the call.

'Another Cannes party,' Anna said. 'Boat ride over to the islands and then a party on the beach.'

'Sounds fun,' Leo said. 'When is it?'

'Later today. I didn't really take in the details as I didn't think we'd be going,' Anna said.

'I'd quite like to see one, if not both, of the islands,' Leo said.

'Oh Leo I'm sorry, I should have asked you first. I just assumed — I'll phone Bruno back, shall I, and ask him for more details?'

Anna looked at Leo aghast as a sudden thought struck her. 'Do you think Bruno already knows who Felicity really is? Has done more than speak to her on the telephone? Surely he would have told me if he had?'

'You'll have to ask him,' Leo said. 'He did arrive with Verity and Nat last night but I think that was coincidence. I'm sure he'd have told you immediately if he knew her true identity. He seems very fond and protective of you. Anna, about what we were discussing?'

'Okay, I promise I'll think about a meeting with Verity before the end of the Festival,' Anna said. 'Now, can we go down early to Cannes? I think I know the present I'd like to get Cindy but I might have to try a few shops.'

'Go and shower. I'll book a taxi for an hour's time,' Leo said sighing. 'That should give us plenty of time to go shopping before your lawyer's appointment. But Anna, promise me you'll do more than just think about meeting Verity. The time for secrets has gone.'

CHAPTER 19

Anna tried very hard to concentrate on what the lawyer was saying but her gaze kept straying to the small carrier bag she was holding on her lap. She'd found the perfect present in only the second shop they'd tried.

A delicate gold rope necklace with the name Cindy hanging from it. Now gift wrapped and secure in the bag, Anna was trying to decide how to get it to Cindy. She really wanted to give it to her today, her actual birthday, but that would mean calling in at the Wickhams' villa. What if Verity — or even Teddy — was there?

'Ms Carson?'

Anna looked at the lawyer startled, 'I'm sorry. You were saying?'

'Philippe Cambone's will. He altered it recently in your favour but there are certain unusual clauses I have to make you aware of.'

'Unusual clauses?' Anna asked.

The lawyer nodded. 'To put it briefly. Philippe has bequeathed the cottage, the boat 'One Life, One Love' and the boathouse on the island to you.' He paused and looked at the paper in his hands. 'You are free to do what you wish with the boat, although Philippe did express the wish that if you decided not to keep it, you would first offer it to his long-time friend Bruno Peters.'

Again the lawyer hesitated. 'The cottage is slightly more complicated. Legally it will be yours for your lifetime but you are not allowed to sell it. On your death it will revert to the Cambone family and not be passed on to any other family you may have. Unless . . . and on this rather delicate point Philippe Cambone was insistent . . . before your death, it is proven that you and he had a child together. In which case the child will be recognized as his heir and under French law you will be required to bequeath the cottage to him.'

As Anna tried to take in the enormity of what he was saying, the lawyer pushed a bunch of keys across the desk to her. 'Perhaps you'd like to take a look at your new possessions and then come back to see me with any questions you may have. There will of course be the usual French bureaucracy to deal with and paperwork to sign in due course.'

Dazed, Anna picked up the keys and put them in her handbag, before standing and thanking the lawyer for his time. As she and Leo left the building and made their way to the nearby taxi rank she said quietly, 'Philippe clearly hoped his unknown son was about to enter his life.'

Leo took her hand and squeezed it. 'Yes.'

'I don't need a boat. Do you think Bruno will? And the cottage. We're never going to live there are we? Shall I just refuse it? Let it go straight to the Cambones? Let them sort things out with the lawyer?'

'Anna, Anna, calm down,' Leo said. 'Why don't we go across to the island and take a look at things before you decide?'

'Bruno's party tonight,' Anna said impulsively. 'We can slip away and have a quick look around then.'

'You wouldn't rather go alone? Without having a crowd of people around?'

'Maybe we'll go across tomorrow on our own as well. I need to talk to Bruno too,' Anna said. 'Tonight I just want to see the cottage — and the boat.' The boat with the name that summed up her and Philippe's relationship so long ago.

'Let's go back to the villa then,' Leo said

as a taxi drew up alongside. 'We can phone Bruno and get the details.'

Poppy was working in the garden, dead heading some roses when they arrived back at the villa. Leaving Leo to make the phone call to Bruno, Anna took her carrier bag and walked across to see Poppy.

'Hi, no nasty lasting after effects from the party then?' Poppy asked looking at Anna.

'No. I'm fine,' Anna assured her. 'Is Tom still going for a birthday tea with Cindy this afternoon? She's such a sweet child, I've bought her a little present. Could Tom deliver it for me please?'

'No problem,' Poppy said wiping her hands before carefully taking and holding the bag by its handles. 'I'll take it indoors and put it with the present I've bought for him to give her.'

Nat had Cindy with him when Daisy arrived at the café they'd arranged to meet in at the top of rue Saint Antoine, away from the majority of the Festival crowds. Cindy was already tucking into a large dish filled with multi-coloured glacé balls, swirled with cream and chocolate crumbs and topped with two crunchy fan wafers.

'Happy birthday Cindy. That looks yummy,' Daisy said.

'Glad you like the look of it, 'cause I've ordered us one each by way of celebration,' Nat said, pulling her close and kissing her before releasing her and nodding at the hovering waiter. 'Ready for our ice creams s'il vous plaît.'

'Celebration?' Daisy said. 'Cindy's birthday. Anything else?'

'My script is going to be auctioned,' Nat said. 'Teddy has shown it to another couple of producers who both like it. He says the most important thing now is for me to get a top notch agent who can handle things. He gave my name to a leading London agency who are keen to sign me up. I've already had an e-mail asking me to contact them and arrange a meeting for next week.'

'Nat, that's wonderful. Congratulations.' Daisy spooned a mouthful of ice cream. 'I could get addicted to this stuff,' she said before looking up at Nat. 'I've decided I'll get the Festival out of the way and then next week start to plan the future.'

'Which will I hope, include me,' Nat said, squeezing her hand. 'You can always come to the States with me.'

Daisy nodded. 'I could.' She smiled at Nat. 'If you really want me to.'

'I really want you to,' Nat said. 'In fact I —'

'But Mummy says we're going to live in England soon,' Cindy interrupted. 'How will you look after me then, Nat?'

'You won't need me, you'll be at school,' Nat said. 'But I promise to come and visit you.'

'Will you bring Daisy?'

Nat and Daisy laughed as they both said 'Yes' at the same time.

'We promise,' Nat said. 'Now eat your ice cream.'

Daisy looked at Nat. 'What "in fact" were you going to say?'

'I know we've only just met but like I told you the other evening, I can't imagine my future life without you in it. I can't bear the thought of us going our separate ways when the Festival ends. Being on different continents is a definite no-no. I want us to be together. To love each other,' he added, looking at her intently as he spoke.

'Oh Nat. Are you sure . . .' He leant across and silenced her with a gentle kiss. 'Very sure.'

'Ugh, you two are soppy,' Cindy said.

Later as they strolled hand in hand down through the crowded streets towards the Croisette, Daisy asked Nat, 'How are things at your place today?'

'Back to normal,' Nat said with a glance

at Cindy who was holding Daisy's other hand, before mouthing quietly, 'Tell you more later. How's Anna today?'

'Haven't seen her. Poppy was going to go and see if she needed a doctor but . . .' Daisy shrugged.

'Is Anna ill?' Cindy asked. 'I like Anna. She's really nice. Did she eat too much at her party?'

'I think perhaps she did,' Daisy said. 'Now, Cindy, I saw a pretty pink bag in this shop earlier. Would you like me to buy it for your birthday?'

'Ooh pleeease. Pink's my favourite colour and I need a bag for school,' an excited Cindy said when she saw the bag with its silver stars and letters spelling out 'Cannes'.

'Not sure it qualifies as a schoolbag,' Daisy laughed. 'But Mummy can decide about that.'

A short time later, as an excited Cindy handed Daisy her precious bag to look after and clambered on board the carousel, Daisy asked Nat, 'So how are things with the Wickhams then this morning? Last night's problems forgotten?'

'If not forgotten at least not being talked about loudly. And Verity is definitely the Felicity Howell who contacted the Cambones. I overheard Teddy telling her there is no way he intends to pursue the search for his mother now that Philippe is dead and he made Verity promise to stop trying to arrange a meeting between him, the Cambones and this unknown woman who could turn out to be his mother.'

'Poppy doesn't believe me, but things are starting to add up in my mind,' Daisy said. 'I think Teddy Wickham's mother is —'

'Anna,' Nat said quietly.

'You think the same?'

Nat nodded. 'The way she fainted last night when she heard who Felicity Howell really is, makes me think it could be.'

'The thing is — do we tell Verity about our suspicions?' Daisy asked. 'Or wait and see what happens?'

'I don't really think we have any choice but to keep quiet,' Nat said. 'It's none of our business for a start and secondly, we don't have any proof. Besides these things always seem to have a way of working themselves out for the best.'

Daisy sighed. 'I do so want a happy ending — especially for Anna. I really like her.'

When they returned to the villa to collect Tom for Cindy's birthday tea, Poppy gave Cindy the present Anna had left for her.

'Can I open it now?'

'Don't see why not,' Nat said.

Cindy squealed with delight as she saw the necklace with her name hanging from it and insisted on putting it on straight away.

'Is Anna in?' Nat asked Poppy. 'Because if she is, I think you should go and say thank you straight away, Cindy, for such a lovely present.'

'I'll come with you,' Tom said, and the two children raced across the garden towards the villa.

Left alone the three adults looked at each other stunned.

'That's some expensive present for a child you barely know,' Daisy said, voicing all their thoughts. 'It's more like something you'd buy a very special child — a grandchild for instance.'

'Mmm. I wonder what Teddy and Verity will make of it,' Nat said thoughtfully.

'Oh come on you two,' Poppy said. 'This is beginning to sound like some sort of conspiracy theory to me.'

Daisy looked at her sister. 'Just you wait and see.'

CHAPTER 20

Cannes was once again in party mode as Anna and Leo walked along the bord du mer towards the quay that evening. The paparazzi were gathered as usual at the foot of the Palais steps; restaurants and bars were full; glamorous women in impossibly high heeled shoes were stepping into limousines to be chauffeured away to some upmarket establishment along the coast to be wined and dined. International TV crews were everywhere filming, their reporters talking earnestly to cameras trying to convey the frenzied atmosphere around them to audiences on different continents.

Bruno, casual in chinos and black polo shirt, welcomed them aboard the luxury yacht he'd chartered for the evening as the stewardess offered glasses of champagne.

'Anna. Leo. So glad you changed your minds. Should be a fun evening.' He hesitated as he looked at Anna. 'Leo told me what happened last night after I left. Are you all right? I'm struggling to accept it but with that wonderful thing called hindsight, I can definitely see a resemblance between Teddy Wickham and Philippe — and you too actually.' Bruno paused. 'Verity and Teddy are hoping to join us later.'

Anna could feel the panic rising.

'Would you like me to ask them not to come?' Bruno asked.

'What reason could you possibly give them, Bruno? No, Leo and I won't stay too long. Hopefully we'll have left before they arrive. I'm not ready for a confrontation with Teddy Wickham yet.

'Have you spoken to Verity?' she asked. 'Told her you know she's Felicity Howell?'

Bruno shook his head. 'Not yet.'

Anna hesitated before asking, 'Are you going to say anything to Teddy about Philippe? About how close you both were?'

Bruno shook his head. 'Not directly no. After all, Teddy isn't aware that anybody knows his true identity. And without breaking several confidences, I can't tell him. But I may possibly talk in a loud voice when he is within earshot about how friendly Philippe and I were. See if he picks up on it.' Bruno swished the champagne around in his glass before taking a sip and looking at

Anna seriously. 'You're probably the only one who can approach the subject with him — if you choose to do so.'

Anna grimaced. 'From what Verity is saying, there seems very little point.'

'We went to the lawyers this morning,' Leo said. 'Anna is about to become not only a French householder but also the proud owner of a boat.'

'Philippe left you "One Life, One Love"?' Bruno said. 'And the cottage?'

'With certain clauses attached,' Anna said. 'Which I need to talk to you about sometime but not tonight. I've brought the keys to the cottage with me. Leo and I are hoping to have a quick look around tonight. If we disappear that's why,' Anna said.

'Philippe invested a lot of money in that cottage over the years — he always hoped eventually to live there,' Bruno said.

'Yes. He told me once what his dreams were for the place,' Anna said quietly.

More guests began to come aboard and Bruno went to greet them, leaving Anna and Leo to make their way along the deck. A few minutes later the hum of the engines could be heard as the yacht began to manoeuvre off the mooring and make its way towards the island.

Bruno had instructed the skipper to take

the yacht around the bay, 'Give everyone a chance to enjoy the champagne and nibbles,' and it was an hour before the yacht drew up alongside the island's public pontoon and people disembarked.

The caterers had the barbecue a few hundred yards along the beach well under control as they arrived and people were soon tucking into the tuna steaks, lamb seasoned with herbes de Provence and pork chops that were on offer.

Across on the mainland, lights were beginning to shine as twilight began.

'If you've had enough to eat I think we should slip away now to see the cottage,' Leo said. 'Don't want to be stumbling around in the dark. Do you remember its location or do we need to ask Bruno the way?'

'If I remember correctly we need to find the lane that goes around the island and it's one of the few houses along there that has a boathouse,' Anna answered.

The gate to the cottage, when they found it ten minutes later, opened easily and together they walked down the path towards the front door. Leo waited as Anna pushed the key into the lock and turned it before he put his hand on her arm and stopped her.

'I think I'll go and take a look in the boathouse. Have a look at your boat, if that's all right with you? Give you five minutes on your own with your memories. Love you,' and Leo kissed her cheek gently before leaving her to push the door open and enter the cottage.

Inside, Anna pressed a light switch and ceiling spotlights threw a seductive golden ambience over the hall and the sitting room it opened onto.

The room with its Provençal colour scheme and traditional furniture felt warm and inviting. Original paintings lined the wall. Silver-framed photographs stood on the piano in the corner. An Oscar stood on the mantelpiece.

Anna could almost sense Philippe's physical presence in this room: standing in front of the French doors watching the yachts out in the bay; playing the piano for his friends; pulling a log from the basket standing at the side of the granite fireplace and throwing it on the fire; turning to smile at her before pouring a glass of wine from the table in the corner; sitting on the comfy sofa reading to a child.

Stairs from the hallway led both up and down. Trying to rid herself of images of Philippe in the sitting room, Anna went upstairs. Three bedrooms, a modern bath-room. A small box room, its walls decorated with faded nursery characters, empty, save for the old-fashioned wooden cradle in the corner.

Stifling a sob, Anna turned and closed the door, before running back downstairs to the hallway and on down again to the kitchen that occupied the entire ground floor of the cottage.

Taking a glass from the dresser, Anna filled it with tap water and sipped it slowly, trying to regain her composure. The house was beautiful, Philippe had done a brilliant job in restoring it but could she ever live in it — even for brief holidays — with Leo? Wouldn't the memory of Philippe and what might have been, infiltrate everything they did together?

Footsteps sounded upstairs in the hallway. Would Leo like the cottage? Anna rinsed the glass and replaced it on the dresser. 'I'm down in the kitchen. Just coming up,' she called in response to the muffled 'Coo-ee' from upstairs.

'Did you like the boat?' Anna asked as she climbed the stairs to the hallway. 'What sort is — Oh!' For a moment she thought she was hallucinating as she looked at the man standing in front of her. A stranger, yet achingly familiar in so many ways.

'I'm sorry to intrude but I saw the lights were on and I couldn't resist asking if I might have a look around?'

Speechless Anna gestured towards the sitting room and the man smiled his thanks as he held his hand out. 'I guess I should introduce myself I'm —'

'You're Teddy Wickham,' Anna said. 'I recognize you from . . . from a magazine photo,' she added wildly. 'Why do you want to look around?'

'It's just that — that I was a great fan of Philippe Cambone's work and wanted to pay my respects. Are you his caretaker?'

'Sort of,' Anna said, realizing that he was being as economical with the truth as she was.

Suddenly Leo's advice that getting the truth out into the open was the only way to go came into her mind. Lying at this first meeting with Teddy Wickham was the wrong thing to do. But before she could say anything Teddy spoke again.

'It's a lovely place. Sensational views. It would make a wonderful family home,' he said strolling towards the window. 'Do you know what will happen to it now that Philippe is dead?'

Anna shook her head. 'The details still

have to be sorted out. Would you like to see upstairs?'

'Please.'

Her heart thudding in her chest, Anna led the way upstairs. 'This is the largest of the bedrooms, so I suppose you'd call it the master bedroom,' she said. 'The last time I saw it, it definitely didn't look like this. There was only . . .' she stopped, realizing she had been about to say that the only furniture the room contained years ago had been a double bed. Ignoring Teddy's puzzled look she opened the door of the box room.

'This appears to be the only room Philippe hasn't redecorated,' she said. 'Maybe it was next on the list.'

'Hey, I love these old nursery characters,' Teddy said peering at the faded pictures on the wall. 'Looks like a Winnie-the-Pooh theme. As for this cot, it's beautiful.' He fell silent as he carefully pushed the curved rail and it began to gently rock on its runners.

Anna watching him, felt the huge lump in her throat and swallowed hard. She knew she was standing within three feet of the man who, as a baby should have occupied that cradle, of that there was no doubt in her mind. If ever there was a time to speak out it had to be now surely?

'Actually, I'm not the caretaker,' she said

faltering as Teddy turned to look at her.

'Oh?'

'I'm . . . Philippe was an old friend.'

'I was due to meet him for the first time last week,' Teddy said, a sad expression on his face. 'But I left it too late. Everybody I talk to say he was one of life's gentlemen — in every sense of the word.'

'Yes I believe he was,' Anna said quietly. She took a deep breath before continuing. 'I've met your daughter Cindy at the villa where I'm staying. She's a lovely child. You must be very proud. Your wife too — Verity — she came to my party recently.'

'Hang on. Are you Anna Carson? The woman who gave Cindy that expensive birthday present?'

Anna nodded. 'Yes. She offered to lend me her balloon, the helium one, for my party.'

Teddy looked at her incredulously. 'And because of that you spent what must have been a small fortune on a present for her?'

Anna shrank beneath the intensity of his gaze. 'No, not just because of the balloon. I wanted to give her something special — she's such a sweet child. And,' she added quietly, taking another deep breath as she came to a decision. 'Because in another life, my name was Lucinda Ann Carstairs — and yours was Jean-Philippe. And Philippe Cambone intended that cradle to be yours.'

In the silence that followed her words, Anna clutched the pendant around her neck tightly, praying that she had chosen the right moment to speak out. That she had done the right thing. That Teddy would respond favourably to her.

But Teddy had taken a step away from her. His face void of any expression, he said, 'You're Lucinda Ann Carstairs?'

Anna nodded, her whole body taunt with anticipation as she waited for her son to acknowledge her.

'So, that makes you the mother who gave me away and deprived me of knowing my natural father.'

Anna nodded slowly. Several seconds passed before Teddy spoke again. 'As far as I'm concerned you have no right to call yourself my mother. And my daughter doesn't have a grandmother.'

He turned away and left her standing alone in the room that should have been his nursery. Anna listened to his footsteps echoing through the cottage as he ran down the stairs and out into the lane, slamming the door behind him.

CHAPTER 21

'Thanks,' Anna said, wrapping herself in the towel Leo handed her as she climbed out of the pool. 'You're not swimming?'

'No. I've made us some coffee,' Leo answered indicating the cafetière and cups on the patio table. 'We need to talk.'

Ignoring his last words, Anna moved towards the table. 'I've been thinking, how d'you feel about doing some sightseeing over the next few days? I was thinking we could go to Antibes today and have a mooch around. Maybe Monaco tomorrow? There's so much to see down here, we'd be silly not to do some exploring while we're in the area. We could even go over the border to Italy. I've never been to Italy. What d'you think?'

'I think you're trying to avoid the subject but yes we could do some sightseeing if that's what you want — after we've talked.'

Anna sighed, knowing what Leo wanted

to talk about: last night, or rather the consequences of last night. The memory of that meeting with Teddy Wickham in the cottage would remain with her forever. Talking would not erase it from her conscience or alter its impact on her life.

'I meant what I said on the boat coming back, Leo. Teddy Wickham has made up my mind for me,' Anna said quietly. 'The matter is closed. No more soul searching. No more hoping for any sort of reconciliation.' She looked at Leo as she took the cup of coffee he'd poured her. 'Like you've been saying all week, I have to move on. Let my past mistakes go. Get on with my — our — life together.'

'You're not even going to fight to see Cindy then?' Leo asked.

Anna bit her lip. 'No.'

'I know I've been saying leave the past behind but all the same I can't help feeling you should try just once more to get Teddy to listen to the truth,' Leo said. 'Then you will at least know you've done all you could to do the right thing as far as your Jean-Philippe is concerned.'

Leo placed his coffee cup on the table and took Anna's from her before taking hold of her hands. 'I love you and know the kind of person you are — caring, kind and compassionate. Teddy has this picture of you as the hard-hearted woman who didn't care about him from the beginning. A picture I know is simply not true,' Leo paused. 'Verity is clearly on your side. Go and see her. Get her to talk to Teddy. I think he should at least be presented with the evidence that the fault was not all on your side. I can't bear the thought of anybody thinking so badly of the woman I love.'

'Leo, you didn't see the look in Teddy's eyes when he told me he didn't have a mother. He didn't need to tell me how much he hates me — it was all there in his expression.' Anna was silent for several seconds before adding. 'I don't think there is any way through that kind of anger. And I don't think I have the courage to even try.'

Just then the entrance phone for the villa gate buzzed. Leo answered it, turning to look at Anna, before he pressed the button to open the gate and replaced the phone.

'It's Verity. She wants to talk to you.'

'I can't see her now. I'm going to take a shower and get dressed,' Anna said. 'I'm sorry. You'll have to talk to her. Get rid of her,' and Anna ran into the villa leaving Leo to deal with their unexpected visitor.

Upstairs Anna took her time, soaking in the bath rather than having a shower, decid-

239

ing what to wear and then applying her makeup. It was nearly an hour before she went back downstairs, relieved not to hear voices.

'Leo darling I'm sorry I took so long,' she said walking out through the kitchen to the terrace. 'But I'm ready now. Where shall we go . . .' her voice trailed away as she saw Verity sitting with Leo. She turned to go back indoors.

'Anna, listen to what Verity has come to say,' Leo said standing up. 'I'll leave you two alone to talk.'

'Leo, please stay,' Anna said moving across to hold his hand before turning to face Verity. 'Do I call you Verity or Felicity? Did Teddy send you?'

'Most people these days call me Verity and, no,' Verity shook her head, 'Teddy didn't send me. He doesn't know I'm here. In fact he's told me that I'm to sever all contact with you.'

'So, why are you here?' Anna asked.

'Because I like you, Cindy likes you and I know if he'd only give himself the chance to get to know you, Teddy would come to like you too.'

'He told you about our meeting in the cottage last night? Told you what he said? How he made it clear that he wanted nothing to do with me when I told him who I was.'

Verity nodded. 'He told me. He's also saying knowing his father's family will be enough. But I know it won't. Deep down he's desperate to know the whole truth about his past, to know what both his parents were like, to see any family likenesses that have come down through the generations. To know who he truly is.'

Anna gave a wry smile. 'That desire certainly wasn't showing last night. Anyway, how do you propose getting him to change his mind about me?'

Verity shook her head. 'Not me. You. I want you to talk to him.'

'No.'

'Meet him on Saturday morning and tell him your side of the story,' Verity pleaded. 'He'll be at the villa alone — Nat is taking Cindy out and I've promised myself some last minute retail therapy in the rue d'Antibes. You can explain things. I'm sure he'll respond.'

'No,' Anna repeated.

'Anna,' Leo said. 'Don't you think . . .'

Anna shook her head. 'What part of the word "no" do neither of you understand? Teddy would only be meeting me under sufferance and I, the guilty one, and make no mistake I am as guilty in my own eyes as I am in his, would have to try to convince him to listen. And then, to forgive me for something I find as unforgivable as he does.'

Both Verity and Leo looked at her in silence.

'Sorry, but I've finally made up my mind to let the past go and to make the most of the present and the future. Of course I would like nothing more than to get to know Teddy and I long to tell Cindy I am her grandmother. But I can't inflict a grandmother on her who her father detests. It would do nothing but create tension between them, and I'd hate to be the cause of that. I've caused enough unhappiness as it is.'

'Please Anna,' Verity pleaded. 'Try again with Teddy. I know he will eventually respond. As for Cindy, she already adores you.'

Anna shook her head. 'No. Any approach now has to come from Teddy. He has to be ready to listen. But I will make you a promise. If at any time in the future Teddy decides to contact me, I will see him and answer his questions. So I suggest you use your powers of persuasion on him if you really want to help.'

Verity sighed. 'I intend to. Maybe when we're living in England he'll listen to sense.'

She glanced at Anna. 'Are we still going to meet up occasionally? Have lunch?'

'I'd like too,' Anna said. 'But I'm not sure it would be wise. A complete break might be better, besides, I thought Teddy had told you to sever all contact with me?'

'We don't have to tell him do we?' Verity said with a smile. 'Anyway in a few months' time things might have changed. He could want us all to be one big happy family.'

'In my dreams,' Anna said softly. 'In my dreams.'

CHAPTER 22

Saturday morning and Daisy was in the kitchen ready to take Tom to see the whales with Cindy and Nat.

'Tom will be about five minutes,' Poppy said. 'Time for a coffee. Where are you meeting Nat and Cindy?'

'Outside the station,' Daisy replied. 'Just got time to check my e-mails then and talk to you about . . . Oh, I've got one from Ben.'

'And?' Poppy said.

'Not happy,' Daisy said. 'Thinks I'm punishing him for leaving. Wants to talk. Promises to make things up to me.'

'Seems he didn't get the message then.'

'He'll get this one,' Daisy muttered typing furiously. 'Ben, you are wasting your time. I am NOT, repeat NOT going to marry you. I'm not punishing you for leaving me but I've moved on — met someone else, someone special and I'm making plans for my future — without you. I honestly wish you all the best. Have a good life but I'm sorry, I won't be in it.'

'Well that's told him,' Poppy said, reading over her shoulder.

Daisy pressed send and shut down her e-mail programme. Surely that would be the end of things with Ben. She couldn't spell it out any clearer could she?

'I just hope he gets the message this time,' Daisy said.

'So what are these plans you're making?' Poppy asked.

Daisy glanced at her sister. 'Poppy, I need to talk to you about —'

'Have I got time for some toast?' Tom asked, running into the kitchen. 'I'm starving.'

'If you're quick. We've only got a few minutes before we have to leave,' Daisy said.

A shadow passed by the window and Anna appeared in the doorway.

'Good morning, Anna. Coffee?' Poppy offered, holding up the cafetière.

'No thanks. I'm on my way out. I just came to say Leo and I are going over to Antibes later so please don't worry if there's no sign of life in the villa.'

'We're going to Antibes too,' Tom said through a mouthful of toast. 'For Cindy's birthday treat. We're going on the train to see the whales.'

'I'm sure you and Cindy will have lots of fun,' Anna said. 'Come and tell me all about the whales tomorrow.'

'Can I come for a swim as well?' Tom asked.

'Yes of course. Now I'd better get going otherwise my meeting in Cannes will over-run and Leo will be cross with me. Have fun,' Anna said as she left.

'She looks a bit better today,' Poppy said. 'Thought she looked dreadful when I saw her yesterday.'

'Wonder if there have been any developments with Verity and Teddy,' Daisy said. 'Maybe Nat will have some news.' She closed her laptop and stood up. 'Right Tom, time we were going.'

'Hey, what were you going to tell me?' Poppy said.

'Talk later, sis. No time now. Come on, Tom we'd better run if we're not going to be late.'

Nat and Cindy were waiting for them in front of Cannes station and an hour later they were all finding their seats in the ter-racing that surrounded the whale enclosure, waiting for the display to begin. Tom and Cindy were soon excitedly involved with some of the pirates who were encouraging

246

the audience to get into the spirit of the show to come.

'Any news on the long lost son saga?' Daisy asked Nat when she was sure the children were engrossed in the pirate game.

'Heated arguments in the main. Apparently Teddy came face to face with Anna the other evening at some party or other and walked out on her. Verity has spent the last two days trying to persuade him to make contact and learn the truth.'

'Does . . .' Daisy indicated her head at Cindy, 'know what's going on?'

'No,' Nat said. 'She knows Teddy is upset over something but has no idea what it is. One of the arguments was over Teddy insisting that Cindy had to return her necklace but Verity told him that was a definite no-no for Cindy's sake. She hasn't taken it off once yet, she loves it. She simply wouldn't understand why she couldn't keep it. Oh look, the show is about to begin — here come the whales.'

Hours later when they'd seen not only the whales, but dolphins and sea lions performing, watched the baby penguins being fed and Nat had treated them all to lunch, they began to make their way to the exit.

Passing a souvenir shop Cindy said, 'Can we go in there? I want to buy Anna a present.'

Daisy and Nat looked at each other startled, before Nat said, 'Sure, why not? Let's go.'

Once inside the shop Cindy, with Tom's help, decided that Anna would love a whale in a snow scene globe and happily stood in the queue with Daisy to pay for it.

'I love my necklace Anna gave me and will never, ever, ever, forget her,' Cindy said, looking up at Daisy. 'D'you think she'll remember me for always and always?'

'Oh Cindy love, I'm sure Anna will always remember you. And every time she shakes the globe she'll think about you,' Daisy said, touched by the little girl's obvious sincerity and wondering whether Nat was right when he said Cindy had no idea what her parents were arguing about.

Poppy was in the kitchen when they got back to the cottage late that afternoon. 'Hi guys. How were the whales?'

'They were brilliant, Mum,' Tom said. 'I bought a poster for my room and a pot of sweets for you. Look, there's a picture of a whale on it too.'

'Thank you,' Poppy said.

'Can I go and see Anna, please?' Cindy

said. 'I want to give her the present I've got her.'

'Oh Cindy love, she's not in,' Poppy said. 'Perhaps she'll be back before you leave. If not, you can always leave the present here and I'll give it to her for you.'

Cindy shook her head vigorously. 'No thank you. I want to give it to her myself.'

'Tom, why don't you and Cindy help yourselves to a couple of biscuits and go watch a DVD while I get you something to eat. You will stay for tea, won't you?' Poppy said turning to Nat.

Nat glanced at his watch. 'Can't stay too long. Verity and Teddy are expecting us back. And looking at the black clouds that have followed us home, I think it might rain soon and we haven't got coats with us.'

As the children disappeared to watch a movie, Daisy smiled at Nat. 'I think as birthday treats go, today was a good one for Cindy.'

Nat's mobile buzzed before he could answer. 'Hi Teddy. No, we're actually at Tom's about to have tea.' He was quiet as he listened to Teddy. 'But she's not here anyway,' he said, before falling silent again. 'OK. Twenty minutes then.' He closed the phone before saying, 'Poppy I'm really sorry, but we have to go. Teddy is furious.

Apparently he told Verity to make sure Cindy stayed away from here — something she forget to mention to me. He doesn't want Cindy having any more contact with Anna before we all leave on Monday.'

'How unkind,' Daisy said. 'Cindy adores Anna. They seem to have forged a bond without even knowing about the special relationship they share.'

'I know,' Nat said. 'But Teddy is adamant that their friendship is to stop. I'll just go and get Cindy.'

Daisy and Poppy looked at each other. 'Poor Anna,' they said simultaneously. 'And poor Cindy not being allowed to know her own grandmother,' Daisy added.

'I'm still astonished at that turn of events,' Poppy said.

'Where are the children watching the DVD?' Nat asked, returning to the kitchen. 'They're not in the sitting room. Tom's bedroom?'

Poppy shook her head. 'No. He doesn't have a TV up there.'

She went out into the hallway. 'Tom! Cindy!' she called. 'Where are you?' A clap of thunder was the only response.

Daisy ran upstairs to look. 'No sign of them up there,' she said.

'Tom! I'm getting cross. Wherever you're

hiding, please come out, NOW. Nat and Cindy have to go home,' Poppy shouted.

'Could they have gone across to the villa without us seeing?' Nat asked. 'Hoping that Anna was in after all?'

'If they'd gone out through the boot room, yes,' Poppy answered running towards the back of the cottage. 'This door is usually locked,' she said, staring at the open door swinging in the wind that had arrived with the thunder and the rain that was now bucketing down.

'Right,' Nat said. 'I'll go out this way and check the villa.'

'Here, take this,' Daisy said, grabbing a waterproof jacket from a hook. 'You'll get soaked otherwise.'

'Even if they have gone across to the villa, they can't be inside,' Poppy said. 'Anna and Leo are meticulous about locking up the place when they go out.'

'I'll still take a look,' Nat said and dashed off into the rain.

Together Daisy and Poppy began a thorough search of the cottage. While Daisy searched cupboards, opened wardrobe doors and looked under beds, Poppy braved the small cellar rooms with their large spiders among the electric fuse boxes and discarded suitcases.

'Any sign?' Daisy asked, brushing a cob-web out of her sister's hair as they met up back in the hallway.

Poppy shook her head. 'I don't know what's got into Tom. He normally tells me where he's going to play. Oh good,' she said glancing out of the window. 'Anna and Leo are back. Nat's talking to them and they're going into the villa. Quick, let's go over. Oh dear,' said Poppy, stopping in her tracks. 'Look who's just arrived. Teddy Wickham. I wonder how he's going to react to the news his daughter is missing.'

CHAPTER 23

Anna barely registered the fact that Teddy had arrived, as Nat told her Cindy and Tom were missing. Together with Poppy she started to search the villa room by room, calling out the children's names. 'Cindy! Tom! Please come out, if you're here.'

In the kitchen Leo, ever practical, took charge. 'Right. You've established they're not in the cottage. Anna and Poppy are checking upstairs here. Have you checked the garden? Toolshed, that kind of thing.'

'No tool shed or anything,' Daisy said. 'Just shrubs, the loggia and . . . and the treehouse! I bet that's where they are,' and Daisy ran out into the garden, closely followed by Teddy, Nat and Leo. A crack of thunder just as she reached the foot of the tall parasol pine that the treehouse was built in, made her jump.

'Tom! Cindy! Please come down now,' Daisy shouted. 'The storm is getting closer.

It's not safe for you to be up there.' The wind whipped her words away. 'They're definitely up there,' she said as the three men joined her. 'See, they've pulled the rope ladder up behind them. She stared up at the tree house. 'I don't think they can have heard me.'

'Cindy!' Teddy shouted. 'Come down at once.' When there was no response he turned on Nat angrily. 'What on earth were you thinking of, Nat, letting them go up a tree in the middle of a thunderstorm?'

'It's not Nat's fault,' Poppy said, as she and Anna joined everyone under the tree. 'We all thought they were in the sitting room watching a DVD. I have no idea why they decided to come out here.'

'Well I hope you have an idea of how to get them down now,' Teddy said. 'Do you have a ladder somewhere? Or do we have to call the pompiers?'

Anna moved close to the base of the tree.

'Cindy! Tom!' she shouted as loudly as she could. 'Please come down. We know you're up there. I promise you're not in trouble. We just want to get you indoors safe. Away from this storm.'

Everybody stared upwards, praying for a response from the children but just as Anna said, 'I think we're going to have to find a ladder,' Tom appeared at the front of the tree house and everyone breathed a collective sigh of relief.

'Mum, I'm sorry.'

'Just throw the ladder over, Tom and climb down,' Poppy said. 'Cindy is up there with you, isn't she?'

Tom nodded and pushed the rope ladder over the edge. 'Mum, Cindy climbed up all right but the thunderstorm's frightened her and she says she can't climb down.'

'OK Tom. Well, you come down and one of us will go up for Cindy.'

Once Tom was safely down, Nat went to climb up for Cindy, but Teddy took the rope ladder out of his hands. 'No Nat. I'll go. You hold it steady for me,' and Teddy swiftly climbed up into the treehouse to rescue his daughter. Several minutes passed before he reappeared with Cindy, her face blotched and red from crying, clutching his hand as they prepared to descend.

Anna, watching as Teddy tenderly held Cindy against him while he helped her to climb backwards down the ladder step by step, felt a helpless surge of love swamp her body: her son and her granddaughter. Once they were both safely on the ground it was all she could do to stop herself from rushing forward and hugging them both. Instead she squeezed Leo's hand hard and said, 'Thank goodness everyone is safe.'

'Right, into the kitchen to dry off and hot chocolate all round, I think,' Poppy said. 'And then you two can tell us why you thought climbing up to the treehouse this afternoon was a good idea.'

'Anna, Leo. You going to join us for hot chocolate?'

Anna shook her head. 'No thanks. Leo and I will leave you to it now the children are safe.' Teddy, she knew, would resent being in her presence any longer. 'We'll see you tomorrow. Bye Tom, Cindy. Teddy.' The last name said defiantly, out of politeness.

'Daddy, quick, can I have the bag please?' Cindy said her teeth chattering.

Teddy took a water-stained bag out of his jacket pocket and handed it to Cindy. 'Apparently this is the reason they went into hiding. Cindy wanted to be here when Anna got back. To give her a present.'

'Thank you Cindy,' Anna said, impulsively bending down to give the little girl a hug as she handed her the bag. 'I'm so glad you're safe. Go and get warm now.'

Back in the villa Leo poured them both a glass of wine in lieu of hot chocolate as Anna began to open her present. A knock at the back door surprised them both and

Anna listened as Leo went to answer it.

'May I come in?' Teddy asked. 'Nat is taking Cindy home and,' he hesitated, 'I'd like to talk to Anna.'

CHAPTER 24

'I'm afraid the children's escapade this afternoon was my fault,' Teddy said. 'I thought Verity and I were managing to have our arguments out of earshot of Cindy but apparently not.'

'I guess children don't miss much,' Anna said, not looking at him and continuing to unwrap her present.

'Oh how sweet of Cindy. Look,' and she held up the snow-globe to show Teddy. 'So, why was Cindy so desperate to be here when I got back?'

'She'd overheard me telling Verity not to come here before we leave on Monday and was afraid she wouldn't be allowed to see you again. For some reason she was determined to give you that to remember her by.' Teddy shook his head as he looked the snow scene.

Anna shook the globe and watched the snow falling around the bright pink whale on his blue island before quietly asking, 'Does she know I'm her grandmother?'

'No.' Teddy turned away from her and began to pace around the room.

There was no reply to her quiet, 'Are you going to tell her?' and watching an unresponsive Teddy, Anna nervously shook the globe again. Finally as the silence between them lengthened Anna put the globe down on the table and waited.

Since their encounter in the cottage when Teddy had made plain his feelings towards her, she'd tried so hard to accept his attitude, to convince herself that she was happy to wait for him to come round; that it was pointless to contact him to try to persuade him to listen to her side of the story. But now he was standing in front of her, clearly unhappy, maybe she should try and break the ice — explain a few things?

'Is this your first visit to Cannes?' she asked as he stopped to stare out of the window, his back to her.

'Yes.'

'It's ironic isn't it, that both you and I chose this particular year to come to the festival. Me, to make my peace with Philippe and you to meet your father. Instead, Philippe died and I found myself tormented by the rumours that Philippe's son was in town. And now you're having to deal with meeting the mother who gave you away.'

Anna sighed when Teddy made no response. 'What did you want to talk about?'

Teddy turned to face her. 'Tell me about the man who was my father.'

Anna shook her head. 'I can't. I only knew him for six days. Other people can tell you more than I can. You need to talk to Jacques, to Bruno. They knew him far better than I ever did.' She paused and tidied up the discarded wrapping paper. 'I can tell you about the boy I loved though. He was one of the most kind, tender and humane people I have ever met.'

'OK, tell me about your affair then,' Teddy said.

Anna stared at him. 'It was far, far more than an affair. Philippe was my first, and until I met Leo, my only love.' She fingered the pendant around her neck, wondering where to begin, how to try and make Teddy understand the events of forty years ago.

'For six days we lived only for each other. The in-phrase that year was 'life without limits' and it become our mantra. We knew without question that we were destined to be together for ever, living our lives to the full. I had no reason to suspect when I kissed Philippe goodbye at Cannes station after the Festival was closed, we would never be together again. We'd made so many plans for the future.' Anna bit her lip and swallowed at the memory of her farewell with Philippe before continuing.

'I went back home ready to work my way through the summer to fund my college course and to wait for Philippe to return from the States. I was so looking forward to introducing him to my parents as the man I was going to marry. Six weeks later I realized I was pregnant.'

'Did you tell Philippe?'

'Of course. I wrote and told him. But it wasn't until this week that I learned how pleased he was at the idea of becoming a father and realized how much he cared about me — and you,' Anna said.

'This week?'

Anna nodded. 'Yes. Once my parents knew I was expecting they took control of my life. Which included intercepting my letters. Forty years ago I was led to believe that Philippe had rejected me and our baby. I now know that was a lie.'

'But why didn't you keep me, bring me up on your own — especially if you loved my father as much as you say you did?'

Anna sighed. 'You have to remember,' she said, 'the world was a very different place

261

then. I was just seventeen — still a minor in the eyes of the law and living at home. Legally I couldn't do anything without my parents' consent until I was twenty-one. I couldn't have a bank account in my own name, I couldn't rent anywhere without them standing as guarantors and I had no money to pay rent with anyway. I was also unemployable. It was a world totally alien to the way things are today.' Anna reached for a tissue from the box on the table.

'My parents refused to even entertain the possibility that Philippe would marry me. They said he had used me and that I was stupid to believe he would "make an honest woman of me" to use their old-fashioned phrase. But they promised they would stand by me, let me live at home and finish my education provided I agreed to do as they said.'

Anna was silent as she remembered the terms her parents had imposed. 'I had to go away to an unmarried mother's home, the baby would be adopted and I was never again to mention the subject to them. I fought against having the baby adopted — tried to make them feel guilty about giving away their grandchild. But when I didn't hear from Philippe I had very little choice but to agree to their terms.'

Carefully Anna undid the chain around her neck, opened the pendant and held it out to Teddy. 'This — until three days ago — was all I had left to remind me of you and Philippe.'

Silently Teddy looked at the two pictures in the locket.

'There hasn't been a day when I haven't thought about you; wondered where you were, what you were doing, how you'd turned out,' Anna said quietly. 'If I could have kept you, brought you up, believe me, I would have done. I hate the fact that I had to give you away and Philippe never knew you. But I don't for one minute regret loving him and having his baby.'

'No, the regrets are all on my side,' Teddy said, a bitter edge to his voice, as he snapped the locket shut. 'And missing my father by just a few days is the biggest one of all.' He held the jewellery out to Anna and dropped it into her out stretched hand before turning away from her.

'I suspect not knowing you was one of Philippe's greatest regrets throughout his life,' Anna said, replacing the pendant around her neck. 'But I've come to believe harbouring regrets about the past is a futile exercise. They will poison and ruin the present — and our new relationship — if

you give in to them. We have to move on —
get to know one another as the people our
lives have made of us.'

Teddy turned and stared at her as Anna
struggled to express herself. 'For years I
have listened to friends talk about their
families, their children, unable to mention
my own, unknown son, to anyone. I can't
tell you how happy I am now it's possible
for me to get to know you. For us to be
finally involved in each other's life, to be
friends —'

Teddy held up his hand. 'Stop. I'm not
sure I'm ready to be involved with you. It's
too late for us to play happy families. As for
being friends,' Teddy shrugged his shoulders, 'I don't think we can ever be just
"friends".'

'We could at least try getting to know each
other,' Anna said.

'I have to think about what you've told
me. I also need to try and forgive you for
giving me away, but I'm not sure I can yet.'

'Are you at least going to tell people that
you're Philippe Cambone's son? Lay the rumours that are circulating.'

'I'm not sure,' Teddy said. 'If he was still
alive, yes, but it seems a bit pointless as he'll
never know.'

'If he was still alive, he'd have been shouting about your existence from the top of the Palais des Festivals,' Anna said. 'I know he would have been so proud to have called you his son — as I am. Why should you feel diffident about telling the world he was your father? That I'm your mother,' Anna paused. 'Besides, it's not just about you and me any longer is it? There's Cindy. Are you going to tell her she's got a new grandmother? A grandmother who would very much like to be a part of her life.'

Anna looked at Teddy, inwardly praying that he would respond to her, that he would forgive her and let her into his life. 'Wait here,' she said. 'I have to fetch something I want you to read.'

When she returned, Teddy was just closing his mobile. 'Bruno,' he said. 'He wants to know if I'll consider reading a piece at the memorial service on Monday.'

'Are you going to?'

Teddy shrugged. 'I told him I'd think about it.' Teddy glanced at his watch. 'I have to go. I'm due at the final screening in an hour.'

'Here, take these with you then, but please look after them,' Anna said, holding out the large envelope. 'It's a letter and part of a journal written by Philippe. I think you need to read them. It goes without saying I want them back. They may have only came into my possession a few days ago but they are already treasured. I couldn't bear to lose them.'

'You trust me with them? Aren't you afraid to let them out of your sight?'

'Why wouldn't I trust you with them? You're my son. They were written by your father. They concern you. Hopefully once you've read the envelope's contents you'll feel able to publicly acknowledge Philippe Cambone as your father — and me as your mother.'

CHAPTER 25

Daisy found an empty seat at one of the cafés in front of the rue Felix Faure. Once she'd ordered her cappuccino she opened her notebook and began to write her last Festival report.

'I can barely believe it's nearly a fortnight since I first sat here soaking up the atmosphere as the Film Festival began and now it's virtually over.

'It's Sunday afternoon and the closing ceremony is early this evening. While the last twelve days have been filled with a spectacular amount of glitz and glamour there is now a general feeling of things closing down all around, an air of tiredness hanging about. The crowds on the Croisette have definitely thinned out and bar staff and waiters are beginning to smile again. The hype is almost over for another year.

'Locals are playing boules in front of the restaurants and the usual Sunday afternoon craft fair has assembled around the ornate bandstand. Easels full of paintings by local amateurs, bric-a-brac stalls and tables covered with small antiques are crowded together displaying their offerings, hoping for some celebrity customers before the festival is finally over.

'Italian, Japanese, English, and of course French voices, are everywhere but few people are still wearing their Festival identity badges and I suspect a lot of journalists and others on the fringe of the film industry have already left. Many of the stars who have stayed on for the presentation of the Palm d'Or tonight, are spending the day in Monaco, being entertained and no doubt quaffing vast amounts of champagne as they watch the Grand Prix.

'But, give it another hour and Cannes will be humming again with one last official blast from the Festival organizers. The posh frocks and Jimmy Choos will be being slipped into and on, for the last "walking the walk" up the famous red carpet to hear the announcements and watch the presentation of the ultimate accolade from a film festival.

Speculation is rife as to who will win the Palme d'Or this year, as a clear favourite has failed to emerge during the Festival.

Whoever wins though, is sure of at least one evening of maximum publicity and success at the box office — although that is not always guaranteed if the winning film is deemed to be too arty by the general public.'

Daisy pressed the save button as her mobile rang. 'Hi Nat. Was beginning to wonder where you were. Are you on your way down to meet me?'

' 'Fraid not. I'm over on St. Honorate. It's a long story but basically Verity decided Cindy and I should spend the afternoon over here, out of earshot of the discussion she was planning to have with Teddy.'

'About Anna?'

'Yes. Look I'll see you sometime this evening. Shall I come to the villa or will you be in town for the closing ceremony?'

'Come to the villa. I'm planning to watch the Palm d'Or presentation on television. I've promised Poppy I'll cook lasagne for supper tonight so I'll do enough for you.'

'See you there then. Oh gotta go. Cindy's fallen over. Love you,' and Nat was gone.

Daisy smiled as she switched off her phone, happy at hearing the genuine love in Nat's voice. Opening her notebook again, she read through her report and started to write the last paragraphs.

'As I write this, five or six helicopters are

buzzing across the bay, bringing the stars back from Monte Carlo. The paparazzi still in town, are forming their normal scrum at the foot of the Palais des Festival's red carpeted steps. Fans are taking their places behind barriers, hoping for one last close-up glimpse of a favourite star.

'Once the presentation of the Palm d'Or has been made, the Festival is officially over. Within hours, Cannes will start the process of re-claiming the streets and returning the town to its normal everyday life.

'By midday tomorrow as the marquees are taken down and the huge transporter lorries trundle in and out of town, Festival organizers will already be talking about plans for next year's event. C'est la vie!'

Daisy checked she'd saved the report ready for e-mailing later with details of the winning Palm d'Or film entered and switched off her notebook as a shadow fell across the table.

'Seen the photos of the party I e-mailed over? They should have arrived on your computer by now,' Marcus asked as he placed his cameras on the table and sat down. 'Join me in a glass of wine to celebrate?'

'Celebrate?'

'The end of the Festival and,' he hesitated.

'I've taken a photo of a couple of stars "in flagrante" that should earn me a lot of money.' He shook his head as Daisy looked at him. 'Can't tell you. Top secret I'm afraid for the next couple of days.'

'Oh, OK,' Daisy said. 'I'll look at the photos when I get back to the villa.'

'I've mailed the rest over to Leo and Anna. Just thought you'd like to see the ones of you and Nat.'

'Thanks. Any idea what you're going to do when you get home? Got feelers out for a new job?'

'Got a couple of short-term contracts for some glossy magazine shoots. I'll see what happens after that.' He patted his camera. 'If this photo is the winner I think it's going to be, I won't have to worry for a few months anyway. So, how did you enjoy your first Festival?' Marcus asked.

'It's been great,' Daisy said. 'A real insight into another world. Not a world I'd like to live in permanently but fun to learn about.'

'And of course you've met Nat.'

Daisy smiled. 'Yes — I suppose I have you to thank for that.'

Marcus shrugged. 'He's a nice guy.' He glanced at her. 'If you feel you owe me for the introduction you could —'

'Marcus! Why should I "owe" you anything for introducing me to Nat? In fact you almost derailed things at one point if you remember.'

'Yeah, sorry about that. Just thought you might be willing to share some information.'

'Like?'

'How much did you find out about Philippe Cambone's long lost son in the end?'

'Not much.'

'Did you find out his name?'

Daisy didn't answer as Marcus looked at her speculatively.

'Rumour has it that it's Verity Raymond's husband, Teddy Wickham. Rumour also has it that his mother is in town,' Marcus said.

'I've heard those rumours too,' Daisy said, beginning to gather her things together. There was no way she was going to discuss Anna's business with Marcus.

'The mother wouldn't be the woman I photographed placing a flower outside the restaurant, would it? And whose engagement party I covered at the villa, Anna Carson?'

'I'm sure the truth will leak out eventually,' Daisy said. 'But really, is it anybody's business but the people concerned? The emotional shock for both of them must be huge. I think they have the right to privacy for as long as they want.'

Marcus shook his head at her. 'You had a scoop right on your doorstep, Daisy, and you ignored it. You're really not cut out for investigative journalism are you?'

'No,' Daisy said. 'I don't think I am. I have to go. See you around, Marcus.'

CHAPTER 26

'Are you sure you don't want to go to the ceremony tonight?' Leo asked as he and Anna relaxed on the loungers by the pool, Sunday papers discarded.

'Quite sure,' Anna said. 'Much easier to watch it here on TV. We don't have to dress up for a start! Rick was glad to have the tickets to give to a client and he'll be there to represent us if *Future Promises* should receive an unexpected accolade.'

'Nothing to do then, with having to look at Teddy on stage for an hour?'

Anna shook her head. 'No. Talking of Teddy I hope he hasn't forgotten I want my letter and journal back. We all disappear tomorrow to various parts of the world and I don't want to lose them — not even to Philippe's son.'

'You could always ring Verity. Ask her to make sure they're kept safe until you meet up in England.'

'I think I might do that, if Teddy hasn't returned them by tomorrow afternoon when we're supposed to leave. I'd been praying that after he'd read them, he'd find it easier to come to terms with what happened and contact me. But it's twenty-four hours now and no word.'

'I expect he's been busy,' Leo said. 'Jury duties and all that.'

'Hope that's all it is,' Anna said. 'I have to phone the notaire in the morning and make an appointment. Can we stay another night if he can't see me to tomorrow?'

'No problem for me,' Leo said. 'My next meeting is Friday. But what about Poppy? I expect she's looking forward to getting the villa back to herself.'

'I'll ask her later. We can always go to a hotel — there'll be plenty of empty rooms tomorrow.' Anna shivered and stood up. 'I'm going for a shower. The sun's disappeared and I'm getting cold.'

Later that evening, as they prepared to watch the Festival's closing ceremony on TV, Leo said, 'October tenth is the official start date for the filming of *In the Shadow of Mrs Beaton* isn't it?'

'Yes, provided everything comes together,' Anna said.

'So, could we get married in September

then?' Leo asked quietly. 'September twelfth would be a good day for me.'

Anna smiled. 'Maybe the end of September, the twelfth is a bit too close.'

'September twelfth,' Leo repeated, 'would I think be perfect.'

'Too soon Leo. It doesn't give us enough time to organize things,' Anna said.

'Book the church — I'm hoping here that you want a church wedding and not just a civil ceremony,' Leo said. 'Reception in a nearby hotel. Honeymoon, my secret, my job. End of story.'

Anna laughed. 'What about invitations, bridesmaids, best man, ushers, cars, photographers, cake, flowers, food, wedding dress, hair, going away outfit, shoes, and that is just off the top of my head. Even for a small wedding there's lots of behind the scenes stuff to do.'

'Shall we just run away then? A beach wedding in the Caribbean with a couple of witnesses.'

'No, that wouldn't be us, would it?' Anna said. 'I do see us getting married in a traditional way but three months really isn't very long to prepare for a wedding. For a start your village church may not be available —'

'Oh but it is,' Leo said, picking an envelope up off the table and pulling out a piece of paper. 'Eleven o'clock September twelfth. The marriage of Leo Hunter and Anna Carson will take place at St. Mary's followed by the wedding breakfast at The Woodlands Country Club. The happy couple will depart at five o'clock for a secret destination known only to the bridegroom.'

Anna stared at him stunned. 'When did you arrange all this, Leo?'

'I haven't — totally. These are tentative reservations I made before I came down here knowing I was going to ask you to marry me. Once you'd said yes, I intended picking up the phone and finalizing everything. But,' he paused. 'Things, Teddy, got in the way and I knew I couldn't do it without talking to you first. The options on the church and the country club run out tonight,' he added quietly. 'Can I ring and confirm things? I do so want us to be married.'

'Oh Leo, I do love you,' Anna took a deep breath. 'September twelfth it is then. But I warn you, there's a lot of arranging to be done between now and then.'

'We'll do it together,' Leo said, a happy smile on his face. 'It'll be wonderful, you'll see,' and lovingly he pulled her into his arms and held her tight as he kissed her. 'Right, you'll have to excuse me. I have some very important phone calls to make.'

As Leo picked up his mobile and wandered into the kitchen Anna switched on the television. 'Don't be too long, it's about to start,' she said.

Anna watched as the opening credits of the programme showed a montage of scenes taken throughout the festival: crowds on the Croisette, stars partying, jesters entertaining the crowds, luxury yachts, famous faces smiling, and then the camera panned around to the paparazzi at the foot of the red carpet for the final time.

Last evening or not, the stars were still in full-on glamour mode. Beautiful dresses, jewellery sparkling in the flashlights, dazzling smiles were all there, as the audience for the closing ceremony made their way up the steps. The camera followed the last of the stars as they disappeared into the Palais des Festivals and seconds later the picture changed to a view of the auditorium. The compere introduced the jury as one by one, they made their way to their seats at the side of the stage and the ceremony was underway.

'That's done,' Leo said, joining Anna in the sitting room and handing her a glass of wine. 'September twelfth it is. See, I told you organizing a wedding was easy!'

Anna laughed. 'Let's hope arranging the rest is as easy. Oh, look there's Teddy.' She fell silent as she watched her son take his place on the stage. 'You know, the more I see him, the more I recognize Philippe in him,' she said.

'He has your eyes,' Leo said. 'I hope he has your compassion too.'

Anna sighed. 'Verity seems to think he will eventually accept things. I just wish I could be so sure. Maybe he'll be in touch later tonight when all this hu-ha is over.' She waved her hand in the direction of the TV. 'Or when the lawyer contacts him next week.'

'What are you going to instruct the lawyer to do at your meeting?' Leo asked.

'I want the cottage to go straight to Teddy. I think under French law it has to now anyway — heirs take precedence over everybody else when it comes to inheriting property. I was thinking about the boat too. Unless that has to automatically go to Teddy as well, I think I would like it to go to Bruno, as Philippe suggested.'

'That will leave you with nothing of Philippe's,' Leo said.

'The only inheritance I want from Philippe is for Teddy to acknowledge me as his mother,' Anna said, turning away to concentrate on the TV, inwardly hoping that the camera would show more shots of the jury as the various prizes were announced. More than anything she wanted to soak up pictures of her son, store them in her memory, to be able to recall them in the days ahead but the camera resolutely roamed around, never lingering more than five seconds on any face except for the winners.

'Isn't that Helen the camera is focusing on?' Leo said. 'Sitting next to Rick?'

'Yes. Oh, Leo, I can't believe it. She's won the Prix d'Interprétation Féminine — how wonderful is that for *Future Promises*? Best actress.'

Together they watched as the young actress made her way on to the stage to collect her trophy and make a short acceptance speech in true Oscar winning style.

'I wonder if Teddy knows how deeply you're involved with *Future Promises*?' Leo asked.

'Well he will now,' Anna said. 'Helen has just mentioned my name in her thank you speech, bless her.'

CHAPTER 27

Daisy pushed her laptop across the loggia table and stood up, stretching her arms above her head. 'My time here is done — winner's name entered and final report sent. Wonder if I'll ever report on the Festival again?'

'Why not?' Poppy asked. 'Lots of freelance opportunities around, I would have thought.'

'Depends on the kind of stuff I write — not sure that lifestyle automatically includes entertainment — and also where I end up spending most time I suppose,' Daisy added thoughtfully, looking at Poppy.

'Hey, I've just remembered you never did tell me what you wanted to talk about yesterday.'

'Nat and me.'

'Ahh. Thought it might be. Finally decided he's the one, have you?'

'Given the short time we've known each

other I'm a bit frightened of saying yes, but I think so. I'm still going to give freelancing a try and want to rent the cottage as a base but Nat wants me to go to America with him when he goes. D'you think I should?' Daisy looked anxiously at her sister.

'Definitely. Grab the opportunity — and Nat — with both hands,' Poppy replied. 'Men like him are few and far between. He's almost as nice as my Dan.'

'That good eh?'

'Listen, any man who can make my little sister as happy as you've been recently, gets my vote. You never looked as happy as you do now when you were with Ben.'

'The thing is, and I haven't actually mentioned this to him yet. How d'you feel about Nat moving into the cottage with me? He needs a base somewhere in Europe and the lease of his flat is up soon. He'll need to find somewhere to stay before going to the States.'

'Not a problem,' Poppy said. 'You're both welcome to live here.'

'Great,' Daisy said. 'Oh I forgot to show you these earlier. Look, Marcus e-mailed me some pictures of Nat and me at the party. The rest have gone direct to Anna and Leo.'

'That's a good one of you and Nat,' Poppy

said. 'And this one of you guzzling champagne.'

'I am so not guzzling,' Daisy protested. 'When I saw Marcus earlier he tried pumping me for information about Anna. Don't worry, I didn't tell him anything,' this as Poppy looked at her. 'But the rumours about Teddy Wickham being Philippe Cambone's son are gaining strength. Be interesting to hear if he goes to the memorial service tomorrow. Right, as I'm on kitchen duty tonight, I'd better make a start. Tom eating with us and staying up to watch the fireworks?'

'Yes. Fête day tomorrow so no school,' Poppy glanced at Daisy. 'You sure about staying on for a few days to help me move back into the villa before Dan gets home?'

'So long as we make time to go shopping. Seen some shoes and a bag I covet in one of the shops on the Croisette. Feel the need to treat myself before I start counting the pennies.'

'You'll need more than pennies if you plan to buy stuff from any boutique on the Croisette,' Poppy said.

The cottage door buzzer went. 'That'll be Nat,' Daisy said. 'I'll let him in and he can give me a hand with the lasagne, while I tell him the good news about the cottage.'

Later, after Tom had disappeared indoors to watch a DVD, the three of them sat companionably outside drinking a bottle of wine.

'I can't believe how quickly the last twelve days have gone,' Poppy said. 'I'm glad I was persuaded to rent the villa for the Festival. It's been fun having Anna around. You too,' she said glancing across at Daisy. 'Thanks for your help with everything.

'I'm really looking forward to you both moving in here,' Poppy continued. 'It's going to be great having you around more — in between the two of you jetting off to the States for Nat's work of course. Any idea when you'll go for the first time?'

Nat shook his head. 'No. Could be in a few weeks or a couple of months. My agent just says be ready — and keep working on the next idea.'

'I hope it's not too soon actually,' Daisy said. 'I want to enjoy us being together — and not being tied to office hours for a bit.'

As Poppy stood up to clear the table, Anna and Leo appeared at the cottage gate.

'Hi,' Anna said. 'Can we join you? We want to share our news and celebrate. Helen won best actress tonight and,' she smiled at Leo, 'we've set the date for our wedding.'

'Congratulations on both counts,' Poppy

said. 'Think this calls for champagne. I'll get a bottle.'

'We've brought one over,' Leo said, holding it out. 'Just need glasses.'

'Poppy, before I forget, is it possible for us to stay an extra night?' Anna asked. 'I have to see a notaire before I leave and it will probably be Tuesday before I can get an appointment.'

'Sure. Dan isn't due home until the end of the week. And my parents who were in Monaco for the Grand Prix have decided to stay there for a few more days before coming over here.'

'Have you spoken to Helen since she won best actress?' Daisy asked Anna, as Poppy went to get the glasses.

'No. Rick says she's in a daze. She's been whisked off to some large yacht for an interview and intends to party the night away afterwards. I'll catch up with her tomorrow.'

'So your return to Cannes after all those years has turned out to be a successful one work-wise?'

Anna nodded. 'Yes. The Festival has been great for business. On a personal note, it's a bit mixed,' she grimaced before turning to Nat. 'How is Cindy today? No ill effects from the scare she gave us all yesterday?'

'She's fine. Still refusing to take off her necklace though.'

Anna smiled. 'I expect you've all heard the rumours about Teddy Wickham being Philippe Cambone's son?' Well, they're true — and I am his mother, which as you'll realize makes me Cindy's grandmother.' Anna paused reflectively before continuing.

'Learning of Cindy's existence is one of the two good personal things that has come out of Cannes for me,' Anna said quietly. 'Meeting Teddy Wickham, my son with Philippe, is the other.' She took a glass of champagne from Leo. 'Things are still up in the air but at least certain things are out in the open now. Although it's going to take weeks, if not months, to finally sort things out.' She sighed as she watched the fizzing bubbles in her glass.

'Unfortunately Teddy's not as ecstatic as I am at the news of our relationship but I'm happy finally knowing who he is, what he's doing. Just knowing my son is alive and well after all the years of silence is, I have to tell you, an indescribable joy.' Anna smiled looking across at Leo.

The whoosh of a firework made them all jump and look skywards in time to see red, silver and gold star-bursts explode into the heavens. The display was beginning.

'Right folks, raise your glasses to Helen, star of *Future Promises,*' Leo said. 'And please make a note against September twelfth in your diaries — we expect to see you all in church.'

CHAPTER 28

Anna rang the notaire first thing on Monday and was given an appointment for Tuesday morning. 'At least it means they can start to process the paperwork,' she said to Leo. 'They said I'll probably have to come back at some stage to finalize things but most of it can be done on the computer over the internet.'

'Will they notify Teddy about his inheritance or do you have to?' Leo asked.

'The notaire will do it all officially,' Anna said. 'I must remember to phone Verity before we leave — make sure Teddy has my letter and journal safe. I keep wishing he'd . . .' and her voice trailed away.

'There's still time,' Leo said. 'Perhaps he'll bring them with him to the memorial service.'

'If he comes,' Anna said. 'Maybe he'll decide to boycott the event as he didn't know Philippe.'

Cannes was busy dismantling the trappings of the Festival as Anna and Leo made their way later that day towards the hall where the memorial service was being held. Large trucks lined the road outside the Palais des Festivals as scene shifters went back and forth with forklift trucks loading all the paraphernalia that had been needed to host the Festival.

The huge billboards erected on shop and hotel facades were being removed, while council workers were loading barriers into lorries. Men shouting, loud bangs as metal and wood hit the pavement, combined with the noise of passing traffic made it impossible to talk, as Anna and Leo dodged around the workmen on the Croissette.

The hall, when they arrived, was beginning to fill with people intent on paying their respects to a much-loved colleague. Bruno was standing on the steps and greeted them affectionately.

'Anna. I'm so pleased you're here. I've reserved seats for you and Leo at the front.'

'Oh Bruno I'd rather sit at the back,' Anna protested. 'Surely the Cambones will be at the front?'

Bruno shook his head. 'Only Jacques and his wife. The rest feel that this is very much a tribute from the film industry, which they are not a part of. Ah, here's Verity,' Bruno said. 'Where's Teddy?'

'He's gone back for some papers he forgot. Said to tell you if you still want him to do a reading, he's found a poem he'd be happy to quote from at the end of the service.'

'I am so pleased about that,' Bruno said. 'Now, you'll sit together won't you?' and Bruno led them down through the hall. To Anna's relief the seats, although nearer the front than she would have liked, were to the left and hidden somewhat behind a pillar that offered some privacy. Jacques Cambone was standing to one side and moved forward to kiss Anna's cheek as he saw her.

'Bonjour Anna. I am glad you are here.'

With Verity on one side, and Leo on her other, holding her hand reassuringly, Anna tried to focus on the memorial sheet Bruno had handed her but the picture of Philippe that met her gaze almost had her in tears before the ceremony had even started. As Bruno made his way to the small podium at the front to begin the proceedings, there was still no sign of Teddy.

Although the memorial was not a religious ceremony the tribute did begin with a prayer offering thanks for the life of Philippe Cambone. Afterwards Bruno introduced various friends of Philippe who described their own differing memories of the man who'd clearly had an enthusiasm for life. 'He embraced everything with a passion,' was how one renowned film critic put it. 'He'll be greatly missed.'

Sitting there listening, and occasionally laughing at the reminiscences, Anna could only feel a strange kind of happiness creeping over her, knowing that the man she had loved so passionately all those years ago had inspired so many during his life.

She stiffened, as Bruno, once again taking his place on the podium in front of the congregation to begin to wind up the tributes, was joined this time by Teddy holding an envelope and some papers. Her papers.

Bruno smiled as his initial words were drowned out by a loud bang somewhere in the building, followed by a telephone ringing in an adjacent office.

'I apologize for the "off stage sound effects",' Bruno said. 'But as a film director, I'm sure Philippe would have appreciated them and is probably even now yelling "cut".' He paused.

'We are nearing the end of this official celebration of Philippe Cambone's life. For many of us he will always live on in our memories. However the final tribute today comes from a man who never met Philippe and to him I extend my heartfelt sympathy. I am so sorry he never knew the man who was my best friend, the man who will leave a huge, empty hole in my life.' An emotional Bruno moved away, leaving Teddy alone on the podium.

'As many of you know, I am Teddy Wickham,' Teddy paused. 'I am also Philippe Cambone's son. Unfortunately as Bruno said, I never met my father and until a few days ago I didn't know my natural mother either.' Teddy placed the envelope and papers on the table in front of him and looked around at the audience.

Anna, sitting transfixed at his words, felt a flutter of hope and smiled at Teddy as he looked directly at her before turning his gaze back to the crowd.

'When she did make herself known to me I cruelly rejected her as I believed she'd rejected me all those years ago by giving me up for adoption. There was no way that I was prepared to acknowledge her. Neither did I see any point in telling the world that I was Philippe Cambone's son now that he was dead. My mother gently informed me that he would have been shouting with joy from the rooftops about me. She also told me how much she was looking forward to getting to know her son and her granddaughter. Again, cruelly, I told her that wasn't about to happen.'

Teddy paused and poured himself a glass of water from the carafe someone had thoughtfully provided, before continuing.

'But then two things happened. First, my six year old daughter, Cindy, went missing. Her disappearance for, what, no more than thirty minutes frightened me and made me realize how I would feel if I lost my daughter for real. If all contact was severed. When my daughter was safe, I went to see my mother. She gave me these highly personal papers and a letter that had only just come into her possession, to read.'

Teddy held up the papers briefly before replacing them on the table. 'I have to tell you I cried when I read them.' He was silent for several seconds, before visibly taking a few deep breaths.

Anna, fighting back tears, clutched Leo's hand. 'D'you think he's going to forgive me after all?' she whispered. 'Even announce my name in public?'

Leo squeezed her hand. 'Just listen to what he has to say.'

'The second thing that happened,' Teddy continued. 'Was yesterday I read a poem called *The Gathering* by an unknown author. This poem contains two lines in different verses that stood out and made me question the decisions I was taking.

'The first line "You can open your eyes and see all that I have left" literally urged me to open my eyes and discover my unknown heritage. The second line, further on in the poem, is one I intend to try and live by in the coming weeks as I get to know my birth mother: "You can be happy for tomorrow because of yesterday".' Teddy stopped speaking and looked around at the audience, before once again, looking directly at Anna as he spoke.

'From what has been said here today, I know my father was a popular man. A good man. I will have a lot to live up to as his son, but by acknowledging the woman who is my mother and who was the love of my father's life, I hope I can begin to live up to the expectations I believe Philippe Cambone would have had of me, his son. Thank you.' And picking up his papers, Teddy stepped down from the podium.

Hesitating he turned to look in Anna's direction, and smiled as he saw her already on her feet walking towards him. As she reached his side, Teddy handed her the precious papers. 'Thank you for letting me read these.'

Wordlessly Anna accepted the papers. Taking a deep breath she took hold of Teddy's hand and with Leo and Verity alongside them they left the hall together as mother and son.

With no early morning screening or press conference to attend, Daisy had the luxury of a lie in on Monday morning and it was nearly eleven o'clock before she'd showered and went downstairs.

'Morning Poppy. I could get used to this not working lark,' she said. 'Become a lady of leisure or even a lady wot lunches.' She switched the coffee machine on. 'Coffee for you?'

Poppy shook her head. 'No thanks. Nat just phoned. He's on his way over. Cindy wants to play with Tom one last time apparently before they leave.'

'Thought he wasn't allowed to let Cindy darken our door because of Anna?' Daisy said puzzled.

Poppy shrugged. 'She's not in anyway. He'll be here soon. You can ask him what's changed. Your mobile has been bleeping for the past hour by the way. Your message box must be full.'

Many of the messages were from friends who'd heard about the redundancies at the paper and were offering sympathy. There was one from an editor she'd worked with a couple of years ago asking if she'd be interested in writing some short features and there was one from Ben. A voice message this time, not a text.

Apprehensively Daisy pressed the listen button and held the phone out so Poppy could hear.

'Sorry I messed things up, Daisy. You sound so positive and happy in your e-mails. I really hope things work out for you. I've cancelled my flight back to the UK. I'll stay over here for a bit and see if I can make a go of things. Have a good life. Maybe we'll meet as friends one day. Love Ben.'

'Well that little problem seems to have gone away,' Poppy said. 'Relieved?'

Daisy nodded. 'Yes. I sort of half expected him to turn up here and try to spoil things with Nat.'

The gate buzzer went. 'Here is Nat,' Poppy said pressing the open button. 'Tom, Cindy's here to play.'

'Hi,' Daisy said as Nat gave her a greeting kiss. 'This is a surprise.'

'Cindy was desperate to play with Tom while Teddy and Verity were out this morning. When I rang and Poppy said Anna wasn't here, I thought, why not.'

'Uh oh, you'll be in trouble if Teddy finds

out,' Daisy said.

'I'll face that if it happens,' Nat said. 'With a bit of luck Anna won't return until we've left so I'll be able to assure Teddy that Cindy hasn't had any contact with her.' With the two children playing happily in the pool, Nat and Daisy sat down to watch them and discuss plans for the future.

'When does your job with the Wickhams finish?'

'Officially tomorrow when we get back to the UK. How long you staying on down here?'

'Mum and Dad will be here the day after tomorrow so I want to be here then. Dan gets back at the end of the week. Think I'll probably change my flight to Saturday,' Daisy said. 'Once I get back I'll start putting feelers out for work and packing up the flat. And be back down here in hopefully a month. Ready and waiting for you to arrive for a summer in the sun.'

'Some of the summer might be spent in the States,' Nat said.

'Exciting. When d'you —' Daisy stopped in mid-sentence as she heard the villa gates opening. 'Nat — Anna and Leo have just arrived back. And Teddy and Verity are with them.'

'Cindy, Tom. Out you get,' Nat said.

'Mummy and Daddy are here. Run over to the cottage and we'll get you dry,' and he hurriedly shooed the children in the direction of the cottage where Poppy was waiting with towels and a worried look on her face.

The children were barely dried and dressed when Teddy came over. Everybody tensed, waiting for the explosion.

'Hi kids. Enjoy your swim?'

As everyone looked at him surprised he turned to Nat. 'Would you like to take the rest of the day off? I think we're going to be busy as a family this afternoon. Cindy, say goodbye to Tom. I need you to come to the villa — we have something very important to tell you.'

'OK,' Cindy said. 'Does that mean I'm allowed to see Anna now?'

'Yes,' Teddy said. 'But I don't think you can go on calling her Anna. That is something you and she will need to talk about.'

Watching Teddy walk back towards the villa hand in hand with Cindy, Daisy said, 'Well that sounds as if things on the Anna and Teddy front have sorted themselves out easier and earlier than Anna was expecting. I'm so pleased for Anna.'

EPILOGUE

Four months later. 12 September

Standing in the front bedroom of Leo's cottage, Anna saw Daisy and Nat hand in hand, making their way under the lych-gate and along the path leading to St. Nicholas In The Field church where in half an hour's time she would become Mrs Leo Hunter. Five minutes earlier she'd seen Leo's daughter Alison and her husband tread the same path, and now Poppy and Tom were being welcomed by one of the ushers.

Anna smiled to herself. It was almost unbelievable how things had fallen into place over the past few months just as Leo had insisted they would.

'It's because it's meant to be,' Leo had teased her twenty-four hours before when he'd moved out to a friend's cottage in the village so they could follow the tradition of not seeing each other the night before their wedding.

Downstairs a door banged and thirty seconds later Cindy burst into the bedroom.

'Granny, Granny, we're here. Can I put my dress on?'

'Not until you've given me a cuddle, young lady,' Anna said holding out her arms for Cindy to run into.

'I'm sorry we're late,' Verity said, following Cindy into the room. 'Traffic. Honestly, you'd think we lived fifty miles away not fifteen.'

'No problem. We've got plenty of time. You're looking very glamorous. I love your hat,' Anna said. 'Where's Teddy?'

'He dropped us and walked down to the pub to check on Leo and his best man. Make sure they've got everything — like the rings! He'll be back here soon.'

'Come on then Cindy, let's get you dressed,' Anna said. 'Then you and Mummy can walk to the church and wait for me.

'Cindy, you are the most beautiful flower girl I've ever seen,' Anna said a few minutes later. 'I'm so proud you're mine.' Placing the halo of flowers on to Cindy's head, she gently clipped it into place, before dropping a gentle kiss on the little girl's head. 'Go and have a look in the mirror — see how beautiful you look.'

'Is your dress pink too?' Cindy asked as

she twirled in front of the dressing table mirror.

'No. I did think about a pale pink one but decided it was really your colour,' Anna said, crossing to the large wardrobe and taking her own wedding ensemble out.

'Can I give you a hand dressing?' Verity asked.

'Please. Lots of hidden buttons down the back that I can't reach,' Anna said, slipping the Grecian style gown made in the palest of pale yellow chiffon off its hanger and over her head.

'What d'you think?' she asked anxiously. 'I wanted something special but felt I was a bit too old for a traditional wedding gown.'

'Anna, I'm speechless and I know Leo will be too when he sees you walking towards him. You look amazing,' Verity said. 'Anything in your hair?'

Anna shook her head. 'No. I'm just going to carry a simple posy which is in the kitchen with Cindy's flower basket. Oh I think I can hear Teddy.'

Downstairs, Verity collected the flower basket and she and Cindy kissed Anna before leaving for the church. 'We'll see you there,' Verity said.

Left alone with Teddy, Anna suddenly felt shy and was glad when he took charge.

'We'll give them a head start and then we'll set off,' he said glancing at his watch. 'If we walk slowly you should be a fashionable five minutes late.'

Looking at Teddy, handsome and immaculate in his morning suit, as he checked the cottage doors were locked before they left, Anna felt a sudden rush of happiness.

'Ready?' Teddy handed her the posy of flowers and ushered her out of the cottage, slamming the front door securely behind them. Together they made their way along the path, through the lych-gate and on into the church.

Standing in the church porch as Verity made a couple of last minute adjustments to Anna's dress and Cindy jiggled on one foot desperate to start throwing rose petals, Anna saw Leo waiting for her by the altar.

She turned to Teddy. 'I can't believe how much my life has changed in the past year. When I met Leo I didn't believe things could get any better, and then you happened.' She was silent for a moment. 'We've come a long way in the last few months, haven't we?' she said. 'Who would have thought my own son would be walking me down the aisle to marry the man I love.'

'It's a whole new stage of life for us all,' Teddy said. 'After years of wondering, I know my roots. Now, I'm sure you are going to be very happy married to Leo but, remember, Mum, I'm here if you ever need me.'

Anna smiled tremulously. 'I still can't get used to hearing you call me that, but I do love it so.'

As the organist began a joyful rendition of the 'Wedding March,' Teddy took her by the arm and Anna began her walk down the aisle to marry Leo, at the side of her son and behind her granddaughter joyfully scattering rose petals at her feet.

ABOUT THE AUTHOR

Jennifer Bohnet was born in Weston-Super-Mare and worked as both a bookseller and a landlady, amongst other things, before becoming a full-time writer and moving to France with her husband Richard. She has written a variety of short stories and articles in her time as a freelance writer and her debut novel, *Follow Your Star,* was also published by Robert Hale. For more about the author, please visit her website: www.jenniferbohnet.com